More Critical Praise fo

for *Mouths Don't Speak*

"Gripping and heartbreaking, *Mouths Don't Speak* is an intricate tapestry of familial betrayals, misunderstandings, forgiveness, and love; a testament to the power of new beginnings even after unspeakable tragedies. The pages had me holding my breath!"
—Lauren Francis-Sharma, author of *'Til the Well Runs Dry*

"*Mouths Don't Speak* is an intimate look at the complexities of family separation and bonds, wisdom passed from one generation to the next, and haunting trauma. The 2010 earthquake that ravaged Haiti is seen through different lenses both on the island and across the water in the United States. In the fallout, Katia D. Ulysse weaves a beguiling tale of reverie and colonial imprint, new lives created out of painful pasts, and what it really means to call a place home."
—Morowa Yejidé, author of *Time of the Locust*

for *Drifting*

"An arresting account of the contemporary Haitian-American experience."
—*Publishers Weekly*

"[T]his novel in short stories will appeal to readers of literary and Caribbean fiction."
—*Library Journal*

"Ulysse displaces and redeems her characters with formidable skill, while her precise cuts through all preconceptions. An intense and necessary novel."
—*Booklist*

"Humanity is lost and found in these stories. Ulysse has created a fascinating world of class and cultural distinctions; her stories are engaging."
—*Kirkus Reviews*

"Assimilating qualities of Danticat and Alvarez, Ulysse paints a variegated literary tableau, more sociological than psychological or historical, that translates into fiction the reality, as well as the fragility and vivacity, of life for young Haitian American women of few means."
—*World Literature Today*

"A superb novel in the form of interconnected short stories that follow Haitian families as they move between time and place, before and after the devastating earthquake of 2010."
—*Teaching Tolerance Magazine,* Summer 2015 Staff Pick

"*Drifting* transcends escapism, materialism, and gaudy promises. Ulysse's incisively details her thesis in flashes—short, brisk sentences. This is no easy task, but she pulls it off with flawless ease, sealing her claim to pure artistry. Traversing the Atlantic multiple times, she captures the spirit and letter of the diasporic experience . . . Highly recommended."
—*Jamaica Gleaner*

"Powerful, piercing, and unforgiving . . . Ulysse's prosaic brilliance is unmistakable." —*Kaieteur News* (Guyana)

"Captivating and honest . . . This novel is a win-win for anyone who enjoys character development just as much as plot."
—*The Review Lab* (Columbia College Chicago)

"*Drifting* is an intoxicating account of various short stories by Haitian novelist and literary genius Katia D. Ulysse . . . highly recommended."
—*Black Star News*

"*Drifting* is a remarkable debut by a phenomenal writer. Much like Sandra Cisneros's *The House on Mango Street,* this sublime and powerful book allows us to experience the joys and tragedies of ordinary and extraordinary lives, in small neighborhoods and big cities, in the present and the past. Katia D. Ulysse's talent soars higher and higher to expand both our hearts and our universe." —Edwidge Danticat, author of *Untwine*

"We already know that the Haitian-American community can produce some of our very finest fiction writers. With *Drifting,* Katia D. Ulysse proves that point once again, evoking the immigrant experience with delicacy, gravity, and pathos. Refreshing and arresting on the first read, this book will be remembered for a long time to come."
—Madison Smartt Bell, author of *Behind the Moon*

"In clear prose, Katia D. Ulysse tells the tangled truth of life and brings a sensitive eye to bear on complicated, flawed characters in circumstances at once everyday and extraordinary."
—Michèle Voltaire Marcelin, author of *Lost and Found*

James M. Jave

KATIA D. ULYSSE is a fiction writer, born in Haiti. Her short stories, essays, and Pushcart Prize nominated poetry appear in numerous literary journals. She has been anthologized in *Mozayik: An Anthology in the Haitian Language*, *The Butterfly's Way: Voices from the Haitian Dyaspora in the United States*, and *Haiti Noir*, edited by Edwidge Danticat. She has taught in Baltimore public schools for thirteen years. *Drifting*, a collection of short stories, drew high praise from literary critics. She is the Kratz Center Writer-in-Residence at Goucher College, and she blogs on voicesfromhaiti.com.

MOUTHS DON'T SPEAK

BY KATIA D. ULYSSE

BROOKLYN, NEW YORK, USA
BALLYDEHOB, CO. CORK, IRELAND

For
James, Juliêtte,
Jean-Claude, and Marthe Lucienne

My deepest gratitude to everyone who helped make
this book possible. —Katia D. Ulysse

Published by Akashic Books
©2018 Katia D. Ulysse

ISBN: 978-1-61775-592-7
Library of Congress Control Number: 2017936113

Akashic Books
Brooklyn, New York, USA
Ballydehob, Co. Cork, Ireland
Twitter: @AkashicBooks
Facebook: AkashicBooks
E-mail: info@akashicbooks.com
Website: www.akashicbooks.com

Know that in a former time
Love, sweet love, was thought a crime.
—William Blake

The idols of the nations are silver and gold, made by human hands.
They have mouths, but cannot speak, eyes, but cannot see. They have
ears, but cannot hear, nor is there breath in their mouths.
—Psalm 135: 15–18

ONE

They did not die alone. Black, white, mulatto, quadroon, octoroon, *sacatra*, and *griffe* met the same fate, but there was no comfort in that. Spilt blood ran as red as the Massacre River. Rafael Trujillo would have been tickled pink. Rich and poor; Catholic, Protestant, and Vodouizan would be bound together for eternity. False prophets, missionaries, prostitutes, politicians, kidnappers and their unsuspecting victims, unemployed blacksmiths and prolific journalists, kindhearted beggars and doctors, pacifists, teachers and their students, unborn and still-unnamed children filled dump trucks and wheelbarrows destined for mass graves. Someone said a prayer on that remote mountain range, where a vicious dictator once disappeared those who uttered his name without the proper measure of reverence. The dank smell of despair pervaded the air, as more trucks stacked with corpses arrived. High above the carnage, few clouds obstructed the tranquil sky.

Scalding tears coursed down Jacqueline's cheeks, drenching the front of her faded T-shirt. Across her chest, multicolor paintbrushes leaned against one another, forming the slogan: *No Art. No Peace.* She had not changed her clothes since she learned about the earthquake three days prior. She had not eaten, and she had forgotten to sleep or bathe. She was oblivious to the sickly sweet odor issuing from her pores. What mattered was the near annihilation of her birth country now three thousand miles away from her front door. What mattered even more was finding her family.

The temblor continued to assert its strength by delivering one powerful aftershock after another, destroying whatever hazardous infrastructure existed. Thousands died instantly. Fate took its time with the people trapped underneath slabs of cement, scrawny rebar, and other subpar materials that once supported the multistoried homes built without a hint of a foundation. The capital city, Port-au-Prince, had become ground zero. The final estimate would put the death toll at over a quarter million, but four times that number would be internally displaced: homeless.

Those who were fortunate enough to survive found themselves without food or a drop of drinkable water. Bloodied and dazed, they wandered around the cracked earth, unsure of what to do or where to go. The able-bodied rummaged for anything salvageable to build rudimentary shelters. They collected broomsticks, pieces of corrugated tin, and tree limbs, which they drove into the ground, securing them in place with rocks. Threadbare rugs, flea-infested blankets, and empty plastic sacs emblazoned with the Stars and Stripes and the words *Enriched Long Grain Rice* served as privacy walls. Roofs made of donated blue tarps flapped in the lazy breeze that circulated the oppressive heat, the stench of decaying flesh, and the feeling of utter hopelessness. More *Made in the USA* rice bags covered the dirt floors of these sheds.

Jacqueline dialed her family's home number for what

felt like the hundredth time that day. Although she had never believed in miracles, she was praying now. *Please, God, please.* The call dropped. She sat on the living room couch, her eyes fixed on the television screen.

Port-au-Prince looked like it had been bombed. Stately homes, shanties, and office buildings all collapsed like dominoes, pulverizing their contents, trapping families and employees inside. The victims screamed for help. *We're down here, we're alive!* One anchorman urged the world not to look away: "Hundreds of people are trapped under the rubble. I can hear them—they're talking, they're alive. We tell them we'll help, but we can do only so much with our bare hands. Haiti needs search-and-rescue teams before it's too late."

The famed Cathedral cracked like an egg's delicate shell. School buildings—some five stories high—leaned precariously, as if they were being held up by a single thread. Felled power lines crisscrossed like spiderwebs over heaps of bloated corpses. An old bungalow painted bright blue with red and yellow accents around the windows had stood between two gleaming churches. Now, not one brick remained of the churches but the bungalow looked so pretty and new that it was eerie.

Black arms and fingers, stiffened in death, stretched toward the sky in futile supplication. Moribund eyes flickered then faltered like a faulty recording device, seeing but not seeing—like the pupils of a clay sculpture set out to dry. People carried caskets on their heads and they toted their belongings in small bundles under their arms. They cradled their deceased children. They cried, dried their eyes, and cried again. One man held a photograph of his daughter while he searched for her amongst the sea of disfigured victims strewn in the hospital's parking lot, like totaled vehicles at a junkyard. Someone explained that the hospital was understaffed; the doctors and nurses were doing their best to care for thousands of wounded patients. They had run out of medical supplies and did not know if or when they might receive more. The morgue was full beyond capacity: no one knew the victims' names. The ones who might have been able to identify them were dead too.

Jacqueline wiped her face with the palm of her left hand. Holding her cell phone in her right, she punched a series of numbers. Before a connection could be established, there came three distinct sounds: The first was no sound at all—just a deafening silence that lasted a few spiteful seconds. The next was a *click-click-click*, like a rusty key's teeth being forced into a lock. The third was another empty silence that would have unhinged even the patron saint of patience and understanding.

When the phone rang finally, Jacqueline's heart jumped with anticipation. She shut her eyes and prayed. There was a sound like someone lifting a telephone receiver from its base. "Hello? Hello?" Jacqueline shouted. "Hello—" Before she could draw another breath, the connection was lost. "Hello? Hello!" It was useless. Silence reigned supreme, scornful and interminable.

Jacqueline returned her attention to the television. The anchorman's steel-blue eyes pierced through the screen, seemingly peering into her soul—perhaps they could even read her thoughts. The short-sleeved black T-shirt he wore made his white skin appear translucent. The grave expression on his face matched the messages he delivered, which were burning holes in her heart. It pained her to watch him, but she could not bring herself to look away. The anchorman was her eyes and ears. She needed him to provide her with all the gut-wrenching details which she both feared and needed.

A few moments later, Jacqueline dialed the number again, to no avail. She placed dozen of calls, praying for someone to answer, listening to the vicious silence after each call dropped, and watching the destruction unfold on television. Each day was worse than the last. Each passing hour meant that any information regarding her family would likely be grim. She spent so much time glued to the television that it felt as if the throng of reporters had moved into her apartment. Their identical speech patterns made her wonder if they had been trained by the same broadcast coach/robot. The platinum-haired anchorman relayed the news in a similar tone as his counterparts, but now and again his blue eyes moistened with tears and his voice broke.

Hours went by without Jacqueline shifting her position on the couch. Fear occupied her mind like the needle inside a condemned prisoner's vein; the lethal injection had begun. The walls were closing in, and the weight of reality pressed down on her eyelids. She wanted to stay awake until she heard from her family, but she was exhausted. Her body was failing her.

Suddenly, the anchorman became as animated as a child at the circus seeing for the first time a real-life lion jump through circles of fire without getting burned. Jacqueline bolted upright, wondering what had happened. The camera panned to an elderly woman in the background, covered in dust. She jutted her thumbs upward, singing and waving her arms. Spectators cheered wildly.

They joined the elderly woman in singing a hymn about God and miracles. The anchorman bounced excitedly in his chair; his blue eyes sparkled like Fourth of July fireworks. He said: "The woman you see behind me was buried under the rubble for three days without food or water. She literally walked out of her grave." The camera moved in for a close-up of this person who had spat on Death's face. She smiled triumphantly. "This woman is an example of how resilient Haitian people truly are." From that moment on, "resilient" became the adjective by which Haitians were known. Jacqueline did not feel resilient, though. She was falling apart.

She reached for her cell phone and hit redial, holding her breath and hoping for a miracle of her own. After a number of rings, absolute silence and irritating clicks, the call dropped again. She chided herself for being so irrational as to believe in miracles. After all, the anchorman had said the Florestant Department Store was the first building in the area to collapse. The cameras showed that the roof was on the sidewalk, the neon sign shattered into a thousand pieces, and the shopping carts looked like crumpled bobby pins. Witnesses at the scene reported that only two people had managed to escape before the building collapsed, and one was critically injured. A Good Samaritan put him in his truck and drove to a hospital. The other survivor went on camera to tell the anchorman that there were at least a hundred people—employees and customers—still trapped under the department store. "They're alive. We need to get them out."

Whole neighborhoods mobilized to try and save as many lives as they could, but their arms could not do the work of heavy machinery. Jacqueline felt certain her parents, Paul and Annette Florestant, were among those buried alive under their department store. They were in their sixties and youthful, though not as spry as young people who could leap out of a crumbling building. Still, she placed call after call, hoping against hope to reach them.

Finally, she hit the mute button on the TV's remote control and paced before the images on the screen, looking but not seeing. The cameras offered extreme close-ups of more survivors emerging from their graves. Jacqueline was elated for them and their families, but resented them at the same time. *Why have they risen out of their graves, while others haven't?*

When her cell phone suddenly rang, Jacqueline slid a trembling index finger across the screen to accept the call, a thousand thoughts stomping through her mind.

"Hello?" Her heart was in her throat. At last, she thought, she would find out if her parents were alive and safe.

"Hello, Jacqueline." The voice was low-pitched and foreboding.

"Yes?"

"This is Mr. Jones." Jacqueline's shoulders slumped forward with disappointment. "How are you holding up?" Jones was one of those colleagues with Mister or Miss for a first name.

"All right, I guess," Jacqueline said, already wanting to end the call.

She anticipated that his next question would be: *Has everyone in your family been accounted for?* Her concerned colleagues kept their conversations brief, and always closed with a variation of: *Stay strong, dear; you'll hear something soon.*

We're praying for you; don't forget how resilient you are. And, *If you need anything, don't hesitate to call.*

"Thank you for calling," Jacqueline told Mr. Jones after their brief exchange, and hung up.

The instant she put the phone back in her lap, it rang again. When she heard the voice on the other end of the line, she grimaced.

"Your kids miss you," the man said authoritatively. "They cannot wait for their art teacher to come back, but I told them you might be out for a few more days."

This was one call Jacqueline wished she had sent directly to voice mail. *Why did he tell the kids I would return in a few days?* Her contract stipulated she could receive three days off for bereavement, but this was the sort of unusual circumstance that demanded the rules be studied a little closer. For all he knew, her entire family was dead. She needed time, a lot of it. But she knew her principal was desperate. Every January, without fail, several bright-eyed optimists who couldn't wait to bring their brand of change to inner-city schools back in September quit the job. Sometimes they submitted resignation letters before they left for Christmas break. Sometimes they e-mailed apologies, and sometimes they simply vanished, abandoning their staplers and red pens on their desks. Whatever the method, by some magic their nameplates vanished like monogrammed robes from posh hotels.

The school principal did not have to tell Jacqueline what she already knew: he needed her back at work immediately. "We held a fundraiser for you," he announced a little too cheerfully. "The children emptied their piggy banks; it was all so very touching."

Tears slowly flooded Jacqueline's eyes.

"A buddy of mine who works for a major TV station was excited to learn I have a Haitian on staff—he wants to interview you. I told him I'd arrange it."

Before Jacqueline could protest, the principal continued: "I think it would be excellent for you—you know, cathartic. You would do the interview here at school, of course. I would be by your side. As a matter of fact, our entire school community would go on camera with you—for emotional support."

Jacqueline knew the man enjoyed listening to his own voice. She would not deprive him of this pleasure now.

"You probably saw me on the news this morning," he went on. "The story about the kids' fundraiser practically went viral. I might finally get some real funding to implement a few of my ideas."

"That's wonderful." Jacqueline's tone was flat.

"I definitely recommend you take advantage of that interview, and I suggest you move fast. People want to get a feel for what's happening in Haiti from an actual Haitian." He waited for Jacqueline to speak, but when the silence lasted too long he hurried to fill it: "I think it would be great for you to share your story. This earthquake thing might be in the news for a while, but it won't last forever. Anyway, the students raised two hundred dollars for you and your family. How awesome is that!"

Jacqueline swallowed hard. She knew that in order for her students to collect that much money, they must have skipped meals, emptied piggy banks, and fished out every penny that had fallen inside couches and under their beds.

"Thank them for me," she told the principal, knowing she would never be able to fully express her gratitude, "but I cannot accept the money. Please give it back to them. Let them know how much their concern means to me. Tell them . . ." Her voice trailed off. "I just hope they haven't been watching TV."

The principal laughed. "Did you forget there's no filter in most of these kids' homes? They know everything about everything. Don't worry, though, your colleagues came up with emergency lesson plans to teach concepts like tragedy, poverty, and, of course, Haiti."

Jacqueline agreed with him: there was not much her students hadn't seen. They were old men and women trapped in the bodies of small children. She recalled a sixth grader who was having trouble staying awake in class. When she asked him about his sleeping habits at home, the boy had answered with a frankness that startled her. She had listened attentively while he spoke as if from the sinner's side of a confessional. It was as if he had waited years to tell his story to someone who might care enough to help. Jacqueline was that person.

At first, her student had started speaking slowly, tentatively; but soon, he spun out of control. He could not talk fast enough: "Our apartment got one room. We share the kitchen and bathroom with some other people. Mama works nights. Pops brings a different ho home every single night. They do it in front of us. I tell my sister not to look, but we can still hear their noises."

Jacqueline learned long ago not to interrupt her students when they talked about their experiences. Once they unburdened themselves, she determined whom to call: parents, the school psychologist, or Child Protective Services. The sixth grader continued: "Mama got sick and came home early one night. When Pops hears the keys in the lock, he tells the *puta* to get lost. We got two ways out: the front door and the window. She runs toward the door with no pants on, but Pops grabs her before she can reach it. Mama woulda screamed loud enough for all the saints in heaven to hear. So Pops shoves her out of the window to the fire escape. He locks the window and pulls the blinds down. The *puta's* out there screaming and calling Pops a *maldito perro*. When Mama walks in, she looks half dead 'cause she's so tired. Pops acts all innocent and everything. If Mama was on to him, she didn't say nothing.

"Couple hours later, we hear the loudest knock on the door. Guess who's back?" Jacqueline just shook her head. "*Puta* brings all kinda cops to our place. Pops is so mad the veins on both sides of his head get stretchy. She points ten fingers at Pops, screaming: *That's the motherfucking culo that tried to kill me! Arrest his Mexican ass!*

"Pops coughs like he's so insulted and stuff, you know? He looks at the cops, never at the ho. He says, *First of all, we ain't no Mexicans. Second of all, I ain't never seen that woman in my life. Third of all, why are you people in my house at this late hour?* Mama looks nervous, but she keeps her eyes on Pops.

"The ho makes the sign of the cross, like Pops is some *chupacabra-cipitío-diablo* mix. She says, *This the bitch-ass pinga that pushed me out the goddamn window. Almost broke my fucking legs. I can prove it, my clothes is right by the bed. Let me show you.*"

Jacqueline said nothing as the student continued narrating his story, still speaking quickly, as if he feared he would run out of voice, time, and memory. She nodded her head to let him know he had all the time he needed; she would listen without judging him. The boy drew a long breath. Jacqueline made a mental note to involve the school's social worker immediately.

"Mama's starting to get mad, you could see it on her face. Me and my sister don't even try to breathe. We act like we're invisible, you know? When the ho takes one step forward, Pops starts scratching his head real hard, like he's trying to remember something. *That damn Javier!* He slams a fist on the wall. Everybody is looking at Pops now. He tells the cops he just came from work himself, and the cops look at him sideways. *Tio Javier did it*, Pops explains. We don't got no Tio Javier, but Mama don't even flinch. Pops says: *Ever since we was kids, people say me and him look like twins.*

"Where can we find this Tio Javier now? one cop asks. Pops scratches his head again. *That* loco *is probably a hundred miles away. If you catch him, you have my permission to lock his ass up.* The ho is shaking her head from side to side, 'cause obviously Pops is lying. She tries to get into the house, but Pops blocks her, saying: *Unless you gentlemen got a search warrant, I suggest you leave.* The cops seen how sweet and tired Mama is, so they take pity on her. They already know she's gonna back Pops up. And that was that."

Jacqueline practiced keeping tears from leaking out of her eyes when she listened to the children's stories. As tragic as this boy's experience was, it was mild compared to others she'd heard since she started teaching in the city. As soon as the students left, she had scheduled a meeting with the social worker to discuss what could be done about his situation, but the earthquake had interrupted her plan. She hoped the social worker would rush to his aid before it was too late.

"I won't take money from the children," Jacqueline now reiterated.

"Fine. I'll give the children their money back," the

principal conceded. "And I'll let my journalist friend know you're turning down the donation. That in itself will make a great story about how resilient Haitians are."

Only a few days earlier, he had called her to his office for a meeting about the sixth grade boy. "He's just lazy," the principal had remarked.

Jacqueline cleared her throat. "That kid's got issues that you and I cannot even fathom. The family is fairly new to this country, they're trying to adjust, and it's hard on the kids. I plan to meet with the social worker to see how we can help."

"There's nothing wrong with that kid," the principal said. "He probably spends the night playing video games or whatever. He's just lazy and doesn't want to learn."

"I disagree," Jacqueline said. "He's got a lot going on at home."

"I've got a lot going on, but I still show up every day and do my job. I get that the kid's from a different country and needs to adjust a little. But don't let him fool you. These kids know exactly how things work here. When in Rome, try to fit in with Romans. I mean, if I had to live in El Salvador for a minute, I'd figure it out. Know what I mean? I can go any place in the world I want, whenever I want, and get along just fine. All I have to do is hit this button right here." He made a sweeping gesture with his hands, indicating the ergonomically correct keyboard and the large computer monitor on his desk. His eyes shone with satisfaction and conceit. "I have a passport to the entire world right here in front of me."

"Really?" Jacqueline feigned a smile.

"Ever heard of Google? I don't have to be in El Salvador to see how things are done down there. I don't have to go to Uganda to understand what those people are going through. I can see it all from here."

Jacqueline took a few calming breaths before responding. She thought about when her husband was overseas, and she had dreaded finding out that he had been killed in combat or by friendly fire. "In other words, you can sit behind your desk and fight alongside the troops in Afghanistan right this minute?"

"In a sense, yes." He didn't blink.

Jacqueline could no longer control the anger in her voice. "My husband will feel like a real jackass for doing three tours in Iraq when he could have stayed home and googled the deployments."

The principal had interlaced his fingers and pressed both thumbs against his chin.

Jacqueline was not through: "Try googling what goes on in a Marine's gut when the guy next to him gets blown up while on the phone with his pregnant wife. Try googling how many emotions parents experience when they're front-row center in Arlington Cemetery, losing their hearing to gun salutes."

The principal was seething with anger, but he managed a weak smile. "That will be all," he had said, eying the door, letting Jacqueline know she was dismissed.

Jacqueline refrained from gossip as a rule, but she was so annoyed after this encounter that she shared the details of the conversation with her classroom assistant. The assistant told one person, who told someone else, who told someone else. The lunch lady overheard two teachers talking, and recounted her version of events: "The principal said all foreigners are lazy and deserve to fail." Someone else broadcasted, "The principal said he won gold in the 200-meter butterfly competition after taking swimming lessons on the Internet." The gym teacher said, "Guess who won Wimbledon this year? Yes, you got it. Our illustrious principal googled the match and beat every opponent." Like brushfire, stories about the principal's virtual triumphs lit up the school's corridors, bathroom stalls, and the employee lounge. Teachers had to cover their mouths to keep from laughing when they saw him in the hallway.

When the gossip reached the principal's ears, he was livid. He summoned Jacqueline to his office for another meeting. This time, instead of talking, he produced an official letter addressed to *Human Resources, the Board of Education*, and possibly Jesus Christ Himself. The letter accused Jacqueline of insubordination, unprofessionalism, and sabotaging students' success. He recommended termination.

All those memories besieged Jacqueline now as she listened to him talk about her family in Haiti. "You are in my prayers," he said before hanging up.

Jacqueline returned her attention to the television screen. The anchorman was joined by another reporter, who introduced the world to an eight-year-old girl named Anaika Saint-Louis.

Anaika's braids and thin face were coated with dust. She raised her small voice heavenward: "God, don't let me die here." A slab of concrete was pinning her in place. The reporter said at least twenty-five other people—Anaika's relatives—were trapped under the same collapsed house. They had stopped screaming long ago. "Help me, God," Anika prayed. When God did not respond, she beseeched her mother: "*Manman*, save me!"

Using a hacksaw, the rescue team tried cutting the pipe pinning Anaika under the house. The rubble shifted, and she let out a piercing scream. Fresh tears mixed with the dust on her face formed little muddy tracks running down to her chin. Someone put a pair of protective glasses on her eyes to keep crumbling debris from blinding her. "God, help me!" Anaika's sobs reverberated around the world.

There was no greater human-interest story than Anaika. People who had never heard of Haiti were now talking about this little girl whose life was in danger.

As she witnessed with horror the events unfolding three thousand miles away, Jacqueline felt as useful as a broken watch. Anaika had become a symbol for hope where there was none. If Anaika survived, Haiti might do the same. If she survived, then—just maybe—Paul and Annette Florestant might be found alive too. Jacqueline did the only thing she could: she telephoned several relief organizations, dug deep into her savings account, and donated as much as she could.

As the hours dragged on, Anaika's screams lowered in pitch and intensity. "I don't want to die, don't let me die," she whispered. Jacqueline wondered how many of the deceased had called on God to save them. Had God heard so many pleas for help that the cacophony had drowned out some of the voices? Jacqueline wondered if her own parents had asked God to save them, and whether or not He had answered their prayers.

As the rescuers continued to labor to free Anaika, Jacqueline thought once again about her students at school. When a child's family was homeless, she tried to find a place for them to live. If they were hungry, she made sure they ate. "Are you some kind of Mother Theresa, Ms. Florestant?" her classroom assistant asked more than once. "If you keep feeding these kids like this, you won't have a nickel left to your name. They'll bleed you dry." Jacqueline never worried about herself in that way. Her salary wasn't much, but she had a nest egg, thanks to her parents.

When Jacqueline looked at Anaika on TV she saw another child, one whose eyes were set farther apart, like a doll's. Her face was not dusty and streaked with muddy tears; her skin was soft and glowing. Her cheeks were plump, not sunken. Her clothes were clean, and smelled of lilac and lavender. Her smile—and she always smiled—was angelic and sweet, and her name was Amber Marshall.

Amber was not in Haiti. She had never been, nor would she ever go. She was safe, and would stay safe—her father would see to that.

A sharp pain stabbed Jacqueline's ribs when her mind conjured the image of Amber pinned under a collapsed house. She shot up from the couch and went to the kitchen, removing the photograph of Amber from the magnet attaching it to the refrigerator door. Jacqueline ran her fingers softly over the image of her little girl curled up under a blanket, with her favorite stuffed animal tucked protectively in her arms.

Clutching the picture, Jacqueline hit the speed-dial button on her cell, and waited for a connection. *Silence. Click-click-click. Silence.* She returned to the couch, leaned back, and closed her eyes. Anaika's rescue attempt was still playing on TV. Someone placed a water bottle near her parched lips; she took a sip then turned her face away. When she cried now, there were no tears.

The world held its breath as rescuers worked constantly until they finally pulled Anaika out of the rubble. Unlike other survivors whose powerful voices carried across the known world, Anaika was too weak to whisper. Her weary eyes opened and closed in a languid manner. She needed days of restorative sleep, and dreams of paradisaical landscapes—not wastelands buried under mountains of broken homes and shattered lives. There was an eruption of applause for another successful rescue. Jacqueline's eyelids collapsed from the weight of grief and joy combined.

TWO

Kevin removed the blanket covering the warm bundle in his arms and shook off the snow before it could melt. Despite the fact that the apartment building was in close proximity to the frosty Chesapeake Bay, the heat from the massive radiators in the lobby reminded him of high noon in Fallujah. The leather laptop case slung over his left shoulder contained his computer and several empty pockets that were supposed to be holding some important documents. The quilted sea-blue duffel bag hanging from his right shoulder depicted a petite lady with a silver hibiscus adorning her bright red hair. Jeweled seashells covered the hint of breasts, and her abnormally small waist dipped into nonexistent hips that slinked down to a fishtail where human legs ought to have been. The Little Mermaid's lips were frozen in a sly smile.

Kevin treaded stealthily, like a soldier on a reconnaissance mission. He would not make a sound. The bundle in his arms had a tendency to be volatile when agitated. The old elevator would make too much noise, so he opted for the stairs, even though their apartment was eight stories above the lobby. Amber would not miss a second of whatever sweet dreams three-year-olds have when they sleep soundly in their fathers' arms.

The sleeping child didn't budge while Kevin climbed the stairs two and sometimes three at a time. When he reached the apartment, he opened the lock as noiselessly as a spy or a hit man. But as soon as they crossed the threshold, Amber awoke as if someone had splashed her with icy water. "Mommy!" she screeched, seeing Jacqueline slumped on the couch. Amber's voice rose several octaves: "Wake up, Mommy!"

Kevin pressed his index finger to his lips and whispered, "Shhhhh, sweetheart, let Mommy rest." He knew his wife had not slept since the afternoon of the earthquake. He stayed awake alongside her at night, holding her and stroking her hair, trying—without much conviction—to reassure her that her family would be found alive and uninjured. Although it had been several years since it was required of him to stay awake and alert for seventy-two-hour stretches, the imprint had remained; his body and mind were still conditioned to operate at peak levels with little or no sleep. Knowing how frantic with worry Jacqueline had been about her family, he wanted nothing more than for her to rest now and find the energy she would need in case the future held more sleepless nights.

"Mommy," Amber continued, ignoring her father's request to be quiet, "wake up!"

It seemed to take all of Jacqueline's power to lift her head from the seat cushion. Her eyes, at half mast, took in the two figures standing in her line of vision. She offered something that might have passed for a smile before dropping her head back on the couch.

Kevin rushed Amber to the kitchen, sat her on a stool, and bent his knees so his eyes would meet hers. "Mommy is very tired," he explained. "We need to let her rest. We can talk to her later, when she's awake."

Amber nodded. "Mommy is tired and needs to rest."

"Exactly. Now, what would my big girl like for dinner?"

"Pizza," Amber piped up excitedly, then remembering her father's words, she whispered, "Pizza."

"Excellent choice," Kevin said with a bow. "One slice of pizza coming right up."

Amber's shoulders rose and fell with a suppressed giggle.

Kevin opened the refrigerator, removed a few slices of pizza from the previous night's pie, and microwaved them on a plate. Dinner was ready within minutes. They sat together at the kitchen table, enjoying pizza and glasses of milk.

After dinner, Kevin filled the bathtub with just enough water to reach Amber's ankles—he'd heard too many stories of children drowning in tubs. He bathed and dressed her in her favorite Little Mermaid pajamas. She applied a glob of toothpaste herself, on the toothbrush adorned with the mermaid's pals—a friendly crab, a colorful fish, and others—all frozen midfrolic in a subaqueous theater. She brushed her teeth, leaving a rivulet of whitish spittle in the sink. Before putting her to bed, Kevin brushed and braided her hair as best he could.

Once Amber was settled between her sea-blue sheets and matching blanket, Kevin lowered himself on the floor next to her bed, keeping his eyes on her as if he feared she would disappear. "Read, Daddy," Amber murmured, already yawning.

In a voice softer than any of his Marine friends could

ever imagine Kevin capable of, he began to read from the worn book: "*Far out in the ocean, where the water is as blue as the prettiest cornflower, and as clear as crystal, it is very, very deep; so deep, indeed, that no cable could fathom it: many church steeples, piled one upon another, would not reach from the ground beneath to the surface of the water above. There dwell the Sea King and his subjects.*"

Amber struggled to stay awake. She wanted to hear more of the story, but she was very tired after a long day of playing with her friends.

"Good night, my beautiful princess," Kevin whispered, and gently kissed his daughter's forehead. "I love you."

Amber stirred under the sea of mermaids and friendly aquatic animals. In a soft whisper of her own came the admonishment: "Don't wake up Mommy."

"I wouldn't dream of it," Kevin answered, smiling.

"I love you, Daddy."

"And I love you more than all the mermaids under all the oceans in the universe."

Kevin looked at his watch and saw that it was not yet eight o'clock. He contemplated going to the harbor for a walk, but decided against it. Jacqueline was asleep, and probably would not open her eyes again until morning. Someone needed to be alert in the apartment with Amber sleeping, in case of an emergency.

He felt cold and his head suddenly ached. In his mind's eye he saw a kid, six or seven years of age, running across an unpaved street. The boy had in his hand what looked like a gun. When the kid disappeared around a corner, Kevin heard shots. Women in burkas chased the boy, screaming in Pashto, as he ran away, panting. He had done his work, and would be paid enough to feed his family for at least one day. Kevin tried to expunge the memory by turning his attention to his wife on the couch, who had spent days searching for her family, not knowing whether they were alive. He saw only the boy with the gun. There was blood on his shirt and a grin on his face. Kevin saw himself now in another country. There were thousands of people in the streets. A man on his knees burned, along with the car tire jammed around his torso. The people were screaming in Creole—their president had been taken from them. Kevin's job was to escort the former priest out of Haiti. The streets of Port-au-Prince ran red with blood, as hot as the desert. He would never forget the stench of human flesh roasting under the noonday sun, and he hoped to never see the island again.

When Jacqueline awoke the next morning, Kevin and Amber had already left. She hated herself for having slept as long as she had, but felt infinitely better than she had since news of the earthquake had reached her. Instinctively, she checked her cell phone for messages and missed calls—there were several of the latter. She scanned the numbers in the call log, and determined that none could have come from her family in Haiti. She placed yet another call to her parents, but was met again with silence and clicks. She paced the perimeter of the apartment like a wounded animal seeking an isolated place to die.

In the kitchen, Jacqueline brewed a pot of coffee, which she poured and drank in great gulps. She returned to her spot before the television screen—watching, hoping, sobbing, and hoping some more.

In contrast, the anchorman looked as if he had not

slept all night. There were dark circles under his piercing blue eyes, but his platinum hair still looked meticulous. He was joined now by a neurosurgeon who reported witnessing amputations and other drastic operations performed without anesthesia and in conditions so dismal that the patients might have been better off praying for miracles instead. He talked about the resilience of the Haitian people, and listed the names of several survivors who emerged alive from their own graves after many days without food or water.

Jacqueline closed her eyes for a moment, praying without meaning to. She suddenly felt nauseous—bile rose to her mouth. She ran to the bathroom, lowered her face close to the toilet, and writhed as she vomited up the coffee. Then she splashed cold water on her face, brushed her teeth, and returned to the living room. As she approached the couch, she heard the name "Anaika," and leapt closer to the screen.

The reporter looked deep into the camera, asking his audience if they remembered Anaika's story. Jacqueline blinked hard: of course she remembered the girl. Who could have forgotten her?

The platinum-haired man explained that the doctors at the facility where Anaika was taken after being pulled out of the rubble were unable to treat her, due to the critical nature of her injuries. They had dispatched her to a facility three hours away, but Anaika Saint-Louis hadn't made it. "She died in route," the reporter said, his practiced inflection dissolving into normal human speech.

Jacqueline doubled over with pain; more bile rose behind her teeth. She ran to the bathroom and vomited again. Anaika had been a symbol for Haiti's future. If an innocent child like her could perish, no one deserved to live. Now she was certain that her parents would never be accounted for.

Jacqueline went to the medicine cabinet and sorted through the collection of jars on the shelves, selecting a pill no bigger than an ant. She swallowed it without water. *Stop fooling yourself, and accept the fact that your family is dead.* A few moments later, the pill kicked in and she felt herself floating above the couch. She was awake and asleep at the same time, and grateful for her semiconscious state.

Jacqueline wondered if her own resiliency had thinned because she'd been out of Haiti for twenty-five years. Those men and women who were buried alive for days, and emerged with a song on their lips and thumbs jutted upward for having spat in Death's face, were resilient—not her. She allowed herself to hope that just maybe her parents were still alive somewhere, spitting in Death's face too. But she knew they were dead. She felt it in her blood.

Jacqueline rubbed her eyes with the hem of her *No Art. No Peace* T-shirt and dialed her parents' telephone number for what felt like the thousandth time. She looked at the television screen, watching truckloads of bodies being dumped hastily into craters in the remote mountain range where dictators used to dispose of their perceived enemies. The unidentifiable corpses were then covered with dirt. No one would ever know who they were. Their families would spend their lives searching for them, wondering if So-and-So was merely lost, wandering in a foreign province without a dime or a place to sleep at night.

Jacqueline's stomach lurched. Her mouth was dry; her skin itched. Another "Is everyone in your family accounted for?" call came. She never explained to anyone that "everyone in her family" comprised just her mother and father. There were no uncles, no cousins, nobody else. Grandparents on both sides had died long before Jacqueline was even born. Her parents' death would make her the last surviving Florestant. Thankfully, she had Kevin and Amber, and thankfully, they were safe and came home every day—although it felt as if she had not seen them in ages.

As the medication continued its work, Jacqueline's mind vacillated between fear and detachment. She eyed the clock: Kevin and Amber would be home soon. She put water in a pot and set it on a burner, adding olive oil and salt. When the water started to boil, she poured in a box of spaghetti that had been in the cupboard for months, always keeping one eye on the television. The dazed people milling about Port-au-Prince now wore toothpaste mustaches to ward off the smell of decomposing bodies and prevent infections—so they believed.

The anchorman reported that the situation on the ground grew worse by the hour. People continued to die from untreated injuries, and the stench of dead bodies trapped under the rubble was overpowering. He also announced that an impressive cast of celebrities had landed: John Travolta, Sean Penn, Wyclef Jean, Brad Pitt and Angelina Jolie, Bill Clinton, George W. Bush, and many others. Nonprofit organizations collected millions in donations, and many countries and other famous celebrities pledged their support.

Haiti would dominate the news for weeks. Then, one after the other, the reporters would trickle out. Other disasters in other countries deserved coverage. Haitians were used to cyclones and mudslides, not earthquakes.

January 12 had taken the country by surprise and provided newspapers with weeks' worth of headlines, but audiences liked variety. And Mother Nature would oblige them. The reporters had to go wherever the tragedy was raw and fresh, and the dead bodies were still warm.

THREE

A month had passed since the earthquake struck, and Jacqueline had yet to return to work. The calls from colleagues inquiring about her family in Haiti had ceased, but the principal still called a few times. When Jacqueline told him she had not heard from her family, and did not plan to return to work—even if standardized testing was on the way—he finally stopped. He told her she could have all the time she needed, and she thanked him.

At this point, Jacqueline had resigned herself to the fact that she would never hear from her parents again. There was no comfort in knowing that she was but one of many thousands going through the same thing.

Being in the apartment now was like being in jail. She desperately needed to break the cycle of constant worrying and placing calls to her parents' house, knowing they would not answer, fearing what she would learn if someone did pick up. She turned off the television, put her coat on top of the clothes she'd worn for days, grabbed a hat, threw the phone in her purse, and left the apartment. She needed to forget about Haiti and the tragedy for a little while. She needed to breathe.

The cold air was invigorating. Jacqueline walked around

the harbor, looking at everything but seeing nothing. Several stores that carried crafts from around the world displayed Haitian art in their windows with signs that promised to send all profits to help earthquake victims. She bought all she could carry, and had more delivered to the apartment. Soon she found herself in front of the Visionary Museum in Fells Point.

Once inside the museum, she gravitated toward a collection of leather masks from Haiti. She purchased a couple. There were also naïf paintings in bright hues depicting a lush countryside, with women in swaying skirts carrying baskets of fruit on their heads. The men wore straw hats and held machetes. She bought one of those too.

One particular sculpture called out to Jacqueline: a little girl made of metal, with a bouquet of metal hibiscus flowers in her hand. Her hair was parted in the middle and braided. The braids were so long that the artist had decided to twirl them into circles, which at a cursory glance looked like horns. It had taken Jacqueline a few minutes of studying the piece to realize it was not a depiction of a fallen angel, but a beautiful girl-child. She liked it, but decided Amber might be terrified. Then Jacqueline saw a collection of colorful seahorses, butterflies, geckos, frogs, swans, and peacocks. She knew Amber would love those, so she purchased a pink seahorse, a yellow butterfly, and a silver-and-blue peacock.

Jacqueline descended the stairs to the coffee shop. There was a line of people ordering convoluted concoctions, which the calm barista made without a bead of sweat on her brow.

While she waited to place her order, Jacqueline perused a cork board with many business cards and flyers pinned to it. One advertisement in particular drew her interest. *Learn Haitian Creole in Four Weeks*, it promised. The instructor's name was Leyla Guerrier.

Jacqueline took a picture of the ad with her cell phone, then ordered her coffee and drank it greedily on the way back to the apartment.

Her home was strangely quiet without the platinum-haired anchorman and his ensemble. It was time to return to her normal routines, if she could recall what those were. It felt as if it had been years since she had thought about anything other than the earthquake, her parents, and Anaika Saint-Louis.

Teaching will have to wait, she told herself. She could not imagine standing before a classroom and pretending to be cheerful when tears still spurted out of her eyes without warning.

Jacqueline was excited at the prospect of relearning her mother tongue. Although only French had been permitted in her childhood home, she spoke Creole by instinct. But all the Creole she had known a quarter of a century ago was now like a pebble at the bottom of the sea: it would take a monumental effort to find it. Compunction about forgetting her mother tongue joined the growing list of emotions she now had about the country she had once sworn never to step foot on again, not even if she had eight more lives remaining.

She stood at the kitchen counter wondering what it would be like to be able to hold a conversation in Creole. She hoped Kevin might be interested in learning the language with her. That way they could practice with each other.

Jacqueline dialed the number from the ad. After a few rings, a friendly voice answered.

"*Bonjou*," Leyla Guerrier said. Her credentials included doctorates in linguistics and French literature at MIT. She gave Jacqueline a list of references she could contact. "You wouldn't want to deal with some nut case."

Leyla spoke with a distinctively Haitian Creole accent. They discussed the particulars, and agreed to meet the following Saturday.

The prospect of learning Creole filled Jacqueline with euphoria. She skipped across the apartment and threw open the door to a room she had not entered since the first day of the earthquake. Standing in the doorway, she eyed the canvas propped on its easel, rows of paints, and a bucket of brushes. She smiled at the light filtering through the window. She sat on the wooden stool and studied the painting she had started before the catastrophe.

As if on cue, the phone in her pocket rang—the number had a 305 area code. She didn't know anyone in Miami, but answered anyway.

"Hello?"

"Hello, Jacqueline? Hello? Can you hear me?" The caller spoke impeccable French.

"Yes. Who is this?" Jacqueline answered in English-accented French.

"Jacqueline, can you hear me?" The voice was vaguely familiar. "*Chéri*, this is . . ."

Jacqueline's hand flew to her mouth and tears bubbled in her eyes. "Annette?" Her voice was tentative.

"Yes, darling, it's me. How's everything with you?"

"Annette?"

"*Oui, chéri*. It's your mother."

"Where are you? Are you okay? Where have you been?"

"Let's just say I'm not dead," Annette Florestant said with a chuckle.

"Do you have food? Water? What happened to you?!"

Annette Florestant kept enough provisions in her house to feed several households for months. She'd always believed in stocking the large pantry with gallons of mineral water, canned goods, and—of course—Grand Marnier, her favorite liqueur. In addition, every tree on the Florestant property bore fruit. There were countless cherry and lemon trees, sixteen kinds of mango trees, soursop, papaya, plantain, and a forest of breadfruit trees. As long as those trees stood, the Florestant household would never know hunger. The profusion of breadfruit trees in Haiti had begun with the colonists, who saw it as a cheap staple to keep slaves in good working condition. For this reason, breadfruit was considered "slave food," or "poor people's food," but not to Annette Florestant. In spite of the fact that she was one of the wealthiest people in Haiti, she never went a week without devouring at least a couple. Their property was nicknamed the Breadfruit House. People asking for directions to fruit vendors in the marketplace would be told, *It's not too far from the Breadfruit House.*

Jacqueline covered the mouthpiece with her palm, not wanting her mother to hear her crying. "I tried calling you a million times, but I couldn't get through. It's so good to hear your voice, Annette. I thought you were . . ." She would not say the word. "How is Paul? How is the house?" She felt an immediate pang of shame for asking this. What did material things matter now?

Jacqueline could hear her mother draw on her cigarette before she announced: "Our house will outlast the Citadel, darling! Paul, well, that's a different story."

"What about him?" Jacqueline asked, afraid of the answer that might come.

"Alive."

"May I speak to him?"

"He's still in the hospital."

Jacqueline tensed.

"Don't worry, he's fine."

"Why is he in the hospital?"

"Because your father's head gets harder with the years."

Jacqueline waited to hear more.

"Paul suspected the employees were stealing from our big store. He had secret cameras installed, and wanted to see the footage. We had plans for dinner with friends in Kenscoff that evening, so I told your father to postpone going to the store. Do you think he listened to me?"

Jacqueline did not answer. A million thoughts buzzed inside her head like angry wasps.

"He went to the store, like the fool he is. Later, he explained that as soon as he felt the first tremor, he knew it was an earthquake. How many times had we been through those things in São Paulo and San Francisco? We were in Osaka in 1995—that was hell. Paul knew immediately, and he screamed for the staff to get out. They retreated into the back rooms instead; they didn't believe your father. You know how those people can be.

"Well, your father would have been better off if he had not tried to save the people. He almost died, you know. Some blocks fell on him, nearly hit his thick head. He would have been killed on the spot. The debris crushed his legs. Luckily, Pachou had driven him to the store, so he was able to rush Paul to the hospital. They had to amputate. But he's fine now."

Jacqueline started to pace the apartment slowly, shaking her head in disbelief.

"It was necessary," Annette intoned matter-of-factly. "He's lucky to be alive. He talks about you all the time."

Jacqueline said nothing.

"By the way, we're here in Miami." Annette drew deeply on the cigarette. "A good friend of ours flew us to Santo Domingo as soon as we got your father stable. The hospitals there are much better, you know, but nowhere near as good as the ones in Miami. We've been here for a couple of weeks now."

Jacqueline's heart tightened. Her parents had been in Miami the entire time and never contacted her?

Annette added: "They had to amputate both legs just above the knees. But otherwise, he's in good shape. He'll be his old nagging self again soon enough. I keep having to tell Paul that he is actually a very lucky man. He doesn't see it that way."

You are both extremely lucky, Jacqueline thought, but kept the words to herself. Of course Paul and Annette Florestant could travel out of Haiti while it imploded. Her parents had powerful friends who owned yachts and jets; the world was theirs. That was what it meant to be a Florestant in the Republic of Haiti. Jacqueline remembered Pachou—the groundskeeper. Her father always preferred to drive himself places, but thank goodness he let someone take him that day. He would have bled to death. Jacqueline also knew that the only reason her father had received medical attention when others did not was because of who he was.

"I've been by your father's side every day since we got here," Annette said with exasperation in her voice. "I'm exhausted. I'm at the house now."

"The house?" Jacqueline was not aware her parents still had a place in Florida.

"The hospital's CEO happens to be a friend. You probably remember him." Annette puffed again on the cigarette. "He and his wife used to come to our house all the time . . . their son played the violin."

Jacqueline's blood ran hot with rage.

"This house is close to the ocean. And you know the ocean air is good for my nerves. I tell you, Jacqueline, that father of yours is certifiable. He's as stubborn as ever. Haiti is in ruins, yet the man cannot wait to get back there. The Florestant house is fine now, but who knows what'll happen tomorrow? I keep telling him now is not a good time to be stuck in our little *patrie*. The people can't stop looting. Most of our stores have been destroyed, and those that have not been touched will be soon enough. Nothing is safe—no decent person is safe. I told Paul that I don't want anything to do with Haiti for a while. That country is finished, as far as I'm concerned. Our *belle vie* is dead. There's not much left, trust me. I told him I'll find a good place for us here by the beach, and we'll stay around for a year or two. And *then* maybe I'll consider returning to Haiti, but not a moment before. Pachou can watch the house; I'm sure there's nothing he would like better. He can keep the squatters from moving in."

Jacqueline resisted the urge to scream. She wanted to ask her mother how she could have been so cruel for not contacting her until now, but she decided to keep quiet.

"Are you there, Jacqueline?"

"Yes."

"Our house is still in perfect condition. The marble floors are as beautiful as always, and the salon is ready to receive royalty. The chandeliers, the piano—everything is just fine." Her mother's voice was calm and crisp. "Pachou was not as lucky of course." Annette took another puff on her cigarette, and laughed drily.

Jacqueline nodded to herself at the mention of Pachou's name. She remembered him always tending to roses, pruning trees, and sweeping the terraces.

"His place collapsed," Annette said in an offhand way. "We're letting him stay in the breakfast room."

"That's good, I guess."

"When can you come visit your father? He wants to see you. If you don't come soon, he'll probably die. You know how childish men can be when they feel the slightest bit ill."

The air around Jacqueline grew denser with each passing second. It was difficult to breathe now. She gritted her teeth.

"How soon can you get here?" her mother asked again.

"I don't think I can," Jacqueline stammered, but recovered quickly. "I don't have childcare for Amber."

"You mean to tell me you don't have someone helping you over there?"

"Kevin and I don't have a maid."

"Who takes care of the little one?"

"We take care of Amber ourselves."

"How is my big girl?" Before Jacqueline had a chance to respond, Annette added, "And how old is she now? Five? Six?"

"Amber is three years old."

"Of course she is—three is a magical number. And born on the Fourth of July too! That Amber is American through and through, isn't she?"

"It's good to know you both survived, and—"

"Jacqueline, darling, it's goodbye time. You see my number on your phone, yes?"

"Yes."

"Save it. I'll tell your father you'll visit soon. He really needs you."

"Well . . ."

"That's wonderful. Let's talk again soon, yes?"

"Yes."

"Before I forget, he's at Baybrook Memorial Hospital. Call him right away." The line went dead before Jacqueline could even say goodbye.

Jacqueline googled *Baybrook Memorial Hospital*, found the number, and dialed. An operator asked for the patient's name. "Paul Florestant," Jacqueline replied. As a matter of habit, she spelled out the last name. A few moments later, she heard his voice. Although she hadn't spoken to her father in at least a year, she recognized it at once.

"Y-e-s," he said, as if the word were multisyllabic. He was obviously sedated. "Yes?" he said again, waiting, then dropped the receiver.

Paul was tired, and frustrated with the inability to scratch the constant itch at the soles of his feet. He was agitated and wanted to scream, but did not have the energy. He could not tell how long it had been since he'd been asleep, or whether he had slept at all. His head ached and something inside him hurt even more, though he would not have been able to pinpoint the pain's exact location. He did recall, however, that a very pretty nurse had made him promise to push the red button at the side of the bed if he needed anything at all. He hit the button, and the nurse materialized within seconds.

"*Oui*, Monsieur Florestant." She spoke French with a distinctively Cuban accent. She and everyone else in the ward were aware of the fact that this patient was close friends with the hospital's CEO and required special attention. She checked the intravenous drip and the needle inserted in Paul's vein. There was at least half of an hour remaining before the bag would need to be replaced. Everything seemed to be in order, but Monsieur Florestant's forehead bore many pleats, letting her know he was uncomfortable. "How's my favorite patient?" she asked.

"Not great," Paul sighed.

The nurse fluffed his pillow, and smiled the smile she usually reserved for patients on the Pediatrics floor. She tilted her head and asked in a practiced saccharine tone: "On a scale of one to ten, how would you rate your pain?"

Paul looked off in the distance. The pain shooting up his thighs did not compare to the lump in his throat. After many tests, the doctors had assured him his throat was healthy, that nothing physical was lodged there, but Paul still insisted something was wrong. "Perhaps it's time to speak to someone," his friend had said. Paul understood the suggestion to mean that a visit with a psychiatrist might be in order.

It was common for trauma victims to forget, at least temporarily, the incident that brought them to the critical care unit, but Paul remembered most of it. The indescribable agony he felt at the moment his legs were crushed came with an auto-delete feature, but every other memory was intact: the instant the earth had shifted underneath his feet and he had ordered his employees to exit the store looped in his mind. They feared and mistrusted him, and were more frightened and suspicious of their boss than of Nature's habitual wickedness. There was not enough time to convince his workers that he'd experienced earthquakes at other places around the globe, that he knew what could happen. "Get out of the building!" he had screamed, but his employees ran farther into the store. He motioned for them to follow him, but they huddled together in the corner and hid behind shelves, frozen with fear. Seconds later, the walls spun as if on a carousel. The front door spun to the back. "Run!" Paul had screamed, but dust clogged his throat. His shirt sleeve got caught in the wrought-iron security gate that made the store impregnable when no one was there. Now he wished he had never had it installed. He could not disentangle himself fast enough. The walls collapsed. The roof collapsed. There were screams. Did *he* scream? There was searing pain, a blinding pain. And then everything went black.

When he opened his eyes again, he heard someone crying, "Jesus said He would come like a thief in the night." But it was not yet night. "Jesus said He would come back to claim what was His." *Haiti was His. He would claim the ones he loved.* "Jesus is back! My Lord is back!" the voice chanted.

Paul had slipped in and out of consciousness. He did not know when a pair of strong hands lifted him from the rubble, put him in the back of a Range Rover, and locked the doors as they sped away. Ten billion people, it seemed, had filled the streets, but Pachou was an expert at negotiating throngs of people in Port-au-Prince. How many times had he gotten caught in the middle of demonstrations for this or that grievance? How many barricades of burning car tires had he averted? As he fled the chaos with his valuable cargo, people jumped on the truck and latched on like lizards. They would go wherever the car was driving to escape the trembling earth.

"How can you do this to me?" a woman shouted, holding her swollen belly. "As much as I love You, God, how can You turn around and do this to me and the baby in my stomach?"

Paul had slipped in and out of consciousness as the Range Rover devoured the road, rolling over lumps Pachou had no time to inspect. All this Paul recalled. He remembered being in a hospital, with the doctors surrounding him and giving him answers to questions he never even asked. "You are Paul Florestant. You live near Kenscoff. There was an earthquake, but you are safe. Your wife, Annette, is safe. We will take good care of you . . ." All he needed to do was nod. He nodded and nodded. The searing pain slowly dissipated, and the doctors' voices became softer, until they floated away like feathers in the wind.

The next time Paul opened his eyes, he had seen different faces: these doctors wore scrubs that were not stained green and red with blood and rot. These doctors addressed him in Spanish, and they knew his name too. They knew where he lived. Some of them looked familiar. They asked him about Annette, and spoke as if they had known Paul for many years. "She's here. She wants to see you," the doctors said in Spanish, which Paul understood. He nodded. Annette was at his side suddenly, like an apparition. She called him *chéri*. He remembered that.

He'd always loved it when she called him *chéri*.

He fell asleep again. For how long, he would never be able to tell. When he opened his eyes this time, the doctors spoke English. He recognized his friend James, who now ran Baybrook Memorial Hospital in Miami. His friend who had danced the rumba at his house, and spent nights lounging under the breadfruit trees on the Florestant property and swimming in the pool.

James smiled cautiously. "Here you are, my friend! You're going to be fine. I'll see to it that you are taken care of."

All this Paul recalled.

And now he wanted to forget everything. He looked at the pretty nurse standing next to his bed. He rubbed his throat with his hands, indicating that the lump had grown even larger.

"On a scale of one to ten, how would you rate your pain?" the nurse asked again.

"Fifty," Paul replied laboriously. "I mean, one hundred."

The nurse patted his wrist gently. She studied the chart on the opposite wall that listed, among other data, the patient's name, date of birth, and the precise time and dosage he received the sedative his doctor had prescribed. "I'll be right back," she promised.

When she returned, she gave him an injection that ushered him to that place where there was no pain, no painful memory—only a Haiti bordered with lush palm trees and a turquoise sea; egrets, flamingoes, and peacocks prancing about luxuriously.

"Sweet dreams," the nurse said, and returned to her station.

FOUR

Jacqueline thought about the father she once knew. She could see him as clearly now as when he towered over her in the grand salon, telling her why practicing the piano another hour was crucial to her upbringing: *Playing well will tell anyone listening that you are refined. They'll know, without a word out of your mouth, that you come from a proper home. No vagabond will dare approach you.*

Jacqueline recalled one Saturday evening long, long ago. Her parents' house was crowded with men in linen suits and ladies in evening gowns that sparkled in the moonlight. Smoke from their cigarettes along with the aroma of roses and jasmine permeated the damp air. Spangly jewels dripped from the women's ears and throats. The men who had danced too closely with the ladies now smelled like them. Their laughter resounded all around—especially in her bedroom, keeping her awake and mildly curious about what they were doing. Servants in white dresses and black aprons served pastries on silver trays. Breezes whipped through the breadfruit trees. Night birds sang saturnine melodies, and cicadas wailed in protest. Annette was resplendent in a ball gown similar to the one the president-for-life's glamorous wife wore on the cover of a popular fashion magazine.

"Don't I look like her?" she asked her girlfriends.

"You look prettier," they said, and Annette smiled. She raised a flute of sparkling champagne, and toasted them.

"*A votre santé*," her guests echoed, raising their own crystal flutes.

They danced and drank. Paul and Annette Florestant were synonymous with elegance, and their parties were as grand as weddings. Friends who were also members of the most popular bands in Haiti brought acoustic guitars, flutes, and saxophones. They played until the morning hours. Jacqueline never even tried to sleep, knowing how the evening would end. It was how the parties always ended: when Annette and her Grand Marnier had had enough of each other, she would summon Jacqueline to the salon and demand that she play "Fantaisie Impromptu." Half-asleep, the child would pound the keys mechanically; but the music delighted the guests.

Then Paul would make a show of taking his wife's hand and kissing it tenderly. The other wives watched in awe, wishing their own husbands would be as sober and sophisticated. They would dab their foreheads with embroidered handkerchiefs. Paul would press the palms of his hands against Annette's lower back, pulling her into him seductively. The other wives would ask for more champagne and curse their own husbands under their breath.

The morning after would be another occasion to celebrate the success of the night that preceded it—every day was a reason for celebration in the Florestant household. Annette contrived any excuse to telephone her girlfriends and throw a party. An hour after her telephone calls, the salon would fill with ladies in Michele Bennet look-alike dresses. Paul, on the other hand, would occupy himself visiting his department stores in Petion-Ville and Port-au-Prince, making sure all was running smoothly and his employees were not stealing the inventory. Then he would drive to a friend's house in one of the most affluent parts of the city. Armed guards patrolling those properties would nod their deference when they saw him. The same guards who had orders to shoot and kill any trespassers would throw the gates open for Paul Florestant.

Jacqueline reached behind the thin gauze covering memories of her youth. She saw her father, the life of every party, so adept at entertaining his guests. She heard samba music, and watched how he glided across the marble floor. His posture was like a vigilant sentinel, but also graceful like Jean-Leon Destiné or Alvin Ailey. His gaze was intense, enigmatic. He danced with Annette and other men's wives skillfully, holding the palm of his left hand steady against their backs, and offering his right hand like a ring bearer's pillow for the women to rest their bejeweled fingers. Each rumba, bachata, or merengue left Paul's clothes smelling faintly of cigarette smoke mixed with orchids, roses, or whatever formula made up the latest and most expensive perfume from Paris. He himself did not smoke, but Annette and many of the other wives did—the president-for-life's wife did too. That made her look chic, sophisticated, worldly. French.

By night's end, Paul's eyes would sparkle like champagne and the rosebud in his lapel would be crushed from the weight of too many intimate embraces. When the dancing was done and guests were looking for their car keys, Monsieur and Madame Florestant would object eloquently, offering bedrooms and promising ambrosial breakfasts.

Now, Paul Florestant, the great dancer, was in the hospital after a catastrophic accident had left him a double amputee. But, as Annette said, he was fortunate to have his life while untold thousands had lost theirs.

Jacqueline promised herself she would call her father the next day. After all, it was late now. Surely the patient needed his rest.

Thousands of miles away from Jacqueline's apartment, Annette flicked her cigarette ashes into the Orrefors ashtray—which had been a gift from her to the homeowner. Annette had purchased it from a shop on the outskirts of Stockholm, Sweden. It had been raining the afternoon she bought it. She had gone into the store, more for shelter than to shop. The clerk had smiled an honest smile when she greeted him in perfect Swedish. She'd stayed in the store long after the rain stopped, and purchased a dozen crystal ashtrays and matching lighters to give as gifts to good friends. Even now, when rain fell, a small part of her traveled back to that little shop near Stockholm. She promised herself she'd return someday.

In the twenty years since that trip, she'd circled the world several times—by ship and by air—passing by Sweden like one going by a neighbor's house without the slightest inclination to knock.

FIVE

"**M**ommy! Mommy!" Amber ran toward Jacqueline with her arms wide open. Jacqueline swept her up in a protective embrace. "I have a surprise for you," the child announced excitedly. "I made it at school."

"I can't wait to see it," Jacqueline replied.

Kevin held up a piece of construction paper with blue feathers and silver glitter glued to it. He brushed Jacqueline's cheek with his lips, whispering in her ear, "Any news?" He noticed the television was off, and wondered if she had finally learned what had happened to her parents.

"They're alive," Jacqueline said with a shrug. To Amber, she said, "I have a surprise for you too, Sunshine. But first, let's have some dinner."

Amber frowned, hoping it would not be a plate of green leaves and carrots. Reading her mind, Jacqueline said, "It's your favorite."

"Yay," Amber clapped her hands. "Pas-get-tee."

Jacqueline set Amber down. "Be a big girl and wash your hands in the bathroom sink." Amber went into the bathroom, stood on the stool, turned on the faucet, and let water fall on her hands for what seemed like an hour.

"So how did you find your parents?" Kevin asked.

"Annette called. Apparently, Monsieur and Madame Florestant have been in sunny Florida the whole time. Annette and the Florestant House are intact, but Paul lost his legs. Annette said that in light of the circumstances, he was lucky. Pachou's house collapsed, so Annette's letting him stay in the breakfast room for now. Monsieur and Madame Florestant plan to relocate to the Sunshine State for an indeterminate length of time. Annette is currently hunting for a suitable place where she and Prince Charming can spend their happily-ever-after."

Amber ran in, taking her favorite chair at the kitchen table. She recounted everything that happened at school, not omitting a single detail. Jacqueline and Kevin appreciated the distraction. After finishing her plate of *pas-get-tee*, Amber convinced her parents to give her a bowl of ice cream with colorful sprinkles on it. A surprising non sequitur followed when Amber said: "I don't want to be a 'geneer anymore, Daddy. I want to be a teacher and a painter like Mommy."

"You are a fantastic painter." Kevin smiled, eyeing the works of art on the refrigerator door.

"Tomorrow, when I go to school, I will make the best painting ever."

"Yes, you will," Jacqueline said as she cleared the table. Then she added: "But tomorrow is Saturday, remember? There's no school on Saturdays."

"Yay!" Amber pumped her fists in the air. "I'm going to help Mommy paint pictures."

"Actually," Kevin said, "I was thinking we could go to the aquarium and then the movies. What do you think?"

Amber reached with both arms around the only part of Kevin she could hold, his neck. "I love the kway-ree-yum, Daddy! I love elephants, and the blue turkeys are my best favorites!"

Kevin chuckled. "Elephants and the blue turkeys are at the zoo, and it's much too cold to go there. We'll visit the aquarium instead." He enunciated the word slowly, for Amber's benefit. "There are no elephants there. As for the blue turkeys, they're called peacocks."

"Peacocks," Amber repeated, but decided she preferred her own description for the large birds, and repeated, "Blue turkeys."

"Well, okay," Kevin conceded. "But there won't be blue turkeys, nor elephants, nor monkeys, not even a koala bear at the aquarium. Only fish, sharks, and slithery snakes, and more fish, and—"

"The Little Mermaid!" Amber piped up.

"You never know." Kevin smiled again. He had to remember she was only three years old.

"Mommy, are you coming with us to the kway-ree-yum?" Amber asked.

Jacqueline started to say something, but Kevin interjected, "Saturdays belong to Mommy, remember? You and I get to leave the house and do whatever we want."

Kevin contemplated his daughter's soft features. She looked a lot like Jacqueline: deep-set brown eyes, a ton of tight-tight curls that fell to her shoulders, and skin the color of honey. Although he never thought of himself as anything but ordinary, in reality his good looks belonged in the movies, and Amber had inherited the best aspects of his features: high cheekbones and dimples that pushed into her cheeks with each smile.

Kevin went to the bathroom and began filling the bathtub for Amber's bath. "Help Mommy in the kitchen while I get your bath ready."

As the water ran, Kevin peered into the next room and

caught sight of his wife and daughter dancing together, as they used to before the earthquake struck. Amber gripped her mother's fingers and twirled like a ballerina in a snow globe. She cackled happily, spinning and declaring, "I love you, Mommy!"

"And I love you all the way to the sky and the moon," Jacqueline replied. Amber's eyes sparkled.

"May I cut in?" Kevin asked.

"Daddy!" Amber exclaimed in a shrill voice. She released her hold on her mother's fingers and ran to Kevin, who swept her up in his arms.

"Isn't it time for her bath?" Jacqueline asked, unamused.

"In a few minutes," Kevin said. "Girls who spend quality time with their fathers grow up feeling loved and confident. Plus, they are less prone to accept some fast boy's version of affection."

Jacqueline agreed with a small nod. Perhaps if she had spent what Kevin called "quality time" with her own father, things might have been different. She might not be married.

After her bath, Kevin wrapped Amber in a fluffy towel with her favorite mermaid emblazoned on it. Then he dressed her in the same pajamas.

Jacqueline walked in with one hand behind her back. She bent down and deposited a kiss on Amber's forehead. When the little girl smiled, Jacqueline brought her hand forward, and presented the seahorse, yellow butterfly, and silvery-blue peacock which she had purchased earlier at the museum. "Here's the surprise I promised you," she said.

Amber reached up, exclaiming, "My blue turkey!" Her

small face arranged itself into the biggest smile Jacqueline and Kevin had seen since the earthquake struck. They looked at one another, chuckling.

Jacqueline took it back from her. "Let's put our friendly bird away for right now. Tomorrow we'll find a spot on the wall to hang all three of them, okay?"

"Okay, Mommy," Amber murmured.

Kevin fluffed the pillow and covered her with the sheet and comforter that made her look like she was a mermaid under water. He never trusted his voice to sing the pretty melody that always put Amber to sleep, so he pressed the play button on the CD player next to the bed. Softly, the voice began: "*Down to the sea we go / Down to a world I know / There's never been, not ever before / A child born of sea and shore . . .*" It wasn't long before Amber began to snore sweetly, and Kevin tiptoed out of the room.

Kevin went into the bathroom, took off his clothes, and stepped into the shower. He sighed deeply as the water cascaded on his face, running to his chin and chest. It had been a long day, though he'd known worse. He recalled days in Fallujah when taking a shower like this was a dream he denied himself. Back then, each shower was like washing his hands and drying them in dirt.

He turned off the faucet when he was done. He dried himself, wrapped the towel around his waist, and went to the bedroom. He took a pair of boxer shorts from a chest of drawers, slipped them on, stretched out on the bed, and fell asleep promptly and deeply—as if in a coma.

Jacqueline was in her painter's studio, sorting through her basket of paints, when someone pounded loudly on the front door, causing Kevin to awaken with a start.

"Goddamnit," he growled.

Jacqueline dropped the tubes of paint and peered into the living room. She knew precisely who was behind the door. How many nights had the person knocked and roused Kevin's anger? *Go to Amber's room and don't come out until I tell you*, he had always told her in the past. She knew this time he would see to it that the stalker never disturbed them again.

Kevin slipped his hand under his side of the bed and grabbed his gun. He peered out the window, hoping to get a look at the man's car, but the heaps of snow eight stories below and low fog in the air made it near impossible to see anything. Smoke billowed from an abandoned row house in the distance. He imagined people screaming and jumping from windows. He thought he heard an explosion, but it was only the pounding on the door.

Kevin threw open the front door and aimed the gun. The man ran quickly down the stairway. There was a woman at the other end of the corridor with a child in her arms. She appeared to be crying. Kevin motioned for her to get back into her own apartment as he rushed downstairs, but the man was already gone.

"Where's Amber?" Kevin asked when he flew back into the apartment—naked except for his boxer shorts.

"In her bed," Jacqueline said. "Sleeping soundly."

She took the gun from her husband's hand and led him back into the bedroom. She hid the weapon under a heap of blankets in the linen closet's uppermost shelf while Kevin went into the bathroom.

He opened the medicine cabinet and removed the prescription bottle that read *Michael Baker* on the label. The pharmacy's address was somewhere in Canada. He shook a couple of pills in his mouth, cupped his hand under the running water, and drank. Then he climbed back into bed, folded his arms on his chest, and waited for sleep to carry him to a different place.

"Those pills work like a dream," Michael had once told Kevin. "The more you take, the better you sleep. It's like being in a coma, except you wake up in the morning."

"What if I don't wake up?" Kevin had asked jokingly.

"Then all your troubles would be over."

"I'm a lot of things, but I am not suicidal," Kevin had countered.

"Nobody said anything about suicide, man. You always take things to another level. Doctors prescribe this medication every day for anxiety and serious insomnia. You think they do that just so people can die? You could kill yourself with half the stuff under your kitchen sink if that's what you want to do. Nobody's trying to die. Personally, I'm done with staying awake twenty-four-seven and feeling like I've got a fucking sniper waiting to take me down, but hey, that's just me."

"I hear what you're saying," Kevin had allowed. "But unlike you, my friend, I have a wife, a child, and a fulltime job. Sleep is not a luxury I can afford; not like you."

Jacqueline entered the room and lowered herself on the bed next to her husband. He stirred and she instinctively put her arm across his chest. Within minutes sleep pressed down on her eyelids like a ton of rubble, but Kevin's eyes stayed fixed on the ceiling: he saw the desert; he saw rows of decapitated palm trees; he saw the boy with the gun and the women crying. He saw himself genuflected before a hooded executioner, hands bound behind his back. Someone held a machete against his neck. The desert sun burned his eyes.

* * *

When morning came, Jacqueline made Kevin's favorite breakfast. She did the same for Amber. She studied the child's eyes, wondering how much she remembered of the night before, but the three-year-old seemed completely oblivious.

When their daughter left the table, Jacqueline whispered to Kevin what she'd been thinking about for some time now: "I don't want that gun in the house, Kevin, even if it's just a Taser. One of these days you'll hurt somebody in that hallway, don't you see? Maybe they'll think you have a real gun and shoot you first. And it's time you went to see a doctor. This self-medicating thing is dangerous."

He chose his words carefully: "Number one, guns don't kill people—people kill people. A Taser is nothing in the real scheme of things. But now that you mention it, I would much prefer to have a firearm in the house. The government has a problem with law-abiding people arming themselves, but any asshole can walk in here and blow up my family if they feel like it. In case you forgot, Baltimore isn't exactly the Garden of Eden. I'm not going to let anything happen to you, and I sure as hell won't let anything happen to Amber. I will certainly not offer my head to a shrink and have that shit on my record like a stain. If my boss finds out, I'll have to explain what's so wrong with me that I need a shrink. I've got it all under control—trust me . . ."

SIX

Jacqueline guarded her Saturdays fiercely. On Saturdays, she became a single woman without a care in the universe. And after the weeks of utter craziness she'd just had, she needed time alone to decompress. Haiti was still in the news, but nowhere near the front pages. There were no more reports about people walking out of their graves. Now, the headlines were about children being distributed to adoptive parents all over the world. A group of missionaries was jailed for trying to smuggle kids across the Dominican border. The news also mentioned that people were now dying from severe diarrhea, vomiting, and dehydration—symptoms associated with cholera. But because that disease had been eradicated in Haiti one hundred years ago, infectious disease specialists were baffled.

The first item on Jacqueline's to-do list was to sequester herself in her small studio to paint. Both Kevin and Amber knew not to disturb her when she painted. She positioned herself in front of the unfinished canvas, contemplated it, and asked herself how to proceed. She picked up her brush, but something churning inside would not let her create. She pondered the possibility of calling her father in the hospital, but then pushed that idea out of her mind. She told herself she would call the next day.

The second item on her to-do list was to call Leyla Guerrier, the Haitian Creole teacher. Relearning Creole would not take long at all, and Jacqueline could not wait.

When Leyla answered the phone, her prospective student explained that although she had been born in Haiti, she had forgotten most of the language because she hadn't spoken it at all in twenty-five years.

"I understand," Leyla said. "I've met many expats in your position. It's great that you want to pick up Creole again."

Jacqueline thought about the teacher's choice of words. She had never considered herself an expat. In order for her to identify as an expatriate, she had to have been a patriot in the first place. Unlike other Haitians who paraded around with the bicolor wrapped around their heads for all to see, she'd never had the urge to follow that trend. She was born in Haiti and spent ten years there. And now she'd lived in the United States of America almost three times as long. As for "picking up Creole again," Jacqueline agreed with the phrase. She did drop Creole, and had no regrets about it. She never planned to return to Haiti.

Leyla said, "People don't want to leave their comfortable homes in this cold, so I have a couple of cancellations. As a matter of fact, the student who was supposed to come this morning texted me from the airport. Guess where he's headed?"

"I don't know," Jacqueline replied.

"Port-au-Prince!" Leyla bellowed. "I told him I didn't blame him one bit."

A pang of shame shot through Jacqueline. Shouldn't she want to travel to Haiti too? They needed help, and wasn't there something she could do to participate in the solution?

"Never mind me," Leyla said. "I have the morning free. It's up to you if you would like to start today."

Eyeing the unfinished canvas, still unsure what to do with it, Jacqueline decided to postpone that work for another time. "Yes, I can make it," she answered. They decided to meet at a coffee shop near Baltimore Harbor.

Jacqueline dressed quickly, and left the apartment without telling Kevin where she was going. When she reached the meeting place, she realized she did not know what Leyla looked like—her picture wasn't on the flyer. Luckily, the coffee shop was probably empty as the weather was so bad. It shouldn't take long to find a Haitian woman sitting alone in such a small place.

Unfortunately for Jacqueline, however, the café was fairly crowded, and there were five or six women enjoying their own company, each leaning into the screen of a laptop. Jacqueline approached a thirty-something woman whose skin was flawless brown. Her brightly colored sweater seemed tropical and incongruous with the cold temperatures. The woman's smile revealed the kind of violet gums men sang about in the Creole folk songs. Jacqueline assumed she had to be Leyla. Conclusive evidence was around the woman's wrist: a blue-and-red rubber bracelet with the Haitian coat of arms at the center.

"Hello?" Jacqueline said politely.

The woman looked up, responding "Hello?" in the same tone.

"I'm Jacqueline."

"Nice to meet you," the lady said. She did not give her own name. Looking around the room and seeing that

most of the chairs were taken, she added, "You're welcome to sit here if you want." She began to gather her
things from the table: her laptop, a coffee mug, a small
plate with the remains of a croissant.

"You're not Leyla, are you?" Jacqueline asked.

"Excuse me?"

"I am sorry to have disturbed you. I'm looking for
someone named Leyla, and silly me, I forgot to ask her
what she looked like."

The lady chuckled. "I understand. I'm not Leyla—not
by a long shot—but I can probably help you out."

"Sure."

The lady went to the counter and spoke loudly enough
for everyone in the room to hear: "If there's a Leyla here, I
recommend you approach the bench immediately. You've
been selected to get a bagel on the house! This offer is
only good for the next five seconds, so come and get it."

Jacqueline shook her head, embarrassed.

"I'm the manager," the lady said. "I can do that."

"Thank you," Jacqueline stammered. "May I ask you
where you got the bracelet?"

"It was a gift from the boss, Leyla." The woman
winked.

"Hi, I'm Leyla," the familiar voice announced softly.
She extended her hand in a businesslike fashion.

Jacqueline turned around, smiling, then could not
conceal her shock. "I'm Jacqueline, it's nice to meet you."

Leyla motioned with her hand toward her table. "Care
to join me?" she said tentatively. "Let's chat for a bit. You
can make up your mind if you want to study Creole with
me or not."

Jacqueline's pants rubbed against the skin on the back

of her thighs and made her itch. The bulky wool sweater she was wearing made her want to scrape off her skin with her nails.

"Coffee?" Leyla started. "We have an extensive menu here, and we carry coffee from all over the world. Of course, my personal favorite comes from Haiti Cherie. That shipment has been delayed, understandably. The Jamaican coffee is pretty good. It comes from the Blue Mountains."

Jacqueline held out her hand. "I'm afraid I've had too much coffee today as it is." She recalled that coffee had been one of Haiti's primary exports in the past, and wondered if that was still the case.

"No problem. Tell me again, why are you interested in learning Creole?"

"Relearning," Jacqueline replied quickly. "I was born in Haiti, and lived there for ten years. Unfortunately, I've been out of the country so long, and, well, there's no one to practice speaking with . . . You know how that is."

"I do know exactly what you mean," Leyla said. "I don't want to forget this beautiful language. I think that's the reason I teach it."

Jacqueline opened her mouth to speak, but Leyla's intense gaze stopped her. The last time Jacqueline had seen eyes so blue was on TV: the platinum-haired anchorman's eyes were identical, and just as piercing. Leyla's hair was not platinum, but a soft shade of blond. Her skin was not as translucent as the anchorman's, but close.

Leyla was used to having to explain how she became a teacher of Creole, so she began voluntarily: "I've always been fascinated with Haiti. The people, the food, the . . ."

She pushed her silky hair behind her ears, leaving her delicate face completely unobstructed. "I lived in Haiti for twenty years. I went there after grad school as a linguist to do some research, and I ended up staying. Luckily, the university had a low-residency program. I was able to study from my adopted home, and submit papers through my trusty e-mail account. Hurray for technology!"

Jacqueline echoed, "Hurray for technology!" As she looked into Leyla's eyes, she likened them to those of a Siberian husky—a sweet puppy, not a wolflike adult. Jacqueline had a sense Leyla could be as sweet as a puppy, and as feral as a wolf when necessary.

"Most people come here expecting to see someone different, but when I show them my credentials, they feel confident that I can get the job done."

Embarrassed once again, Jacqueline offered an explanation of her own: "I saw the name Guerrier, and thought for sure you were Haitian."

"By Haitian you mean to say you didn't figure someone named Leyla Guerrier would have skin so pale. I can't get a tan, even if I lay in the sun all day. I apologize for being so European looking." She laughed.

"I admit it didn't occur to me that you'd have blond hair and eyes so blue."

"Guerrier is my married name. My husband is Haitian. Well, we're divorced now. I liked the name, so I kept it." She motioned for a waitress to approach and placed an order, which Jacqueline did not hear.

Moments later, the waitress returned with an assortment of delicacies, among them *pain patâtte*, *baignets*, *mille-feuilles*, and a sweet roll topped with chunks of *dous makòs*. Jacqueline's eyes widened with surprise. It had been decades since she'd seen *dous makòs*. The fragrant food immediately took her back to her childhood.

"*Manje, pitit, manje mezi vant ou!*" Leyla ordered in a voice as sweet as the array of desserts. "*Se bon bagay peyi w, chéri m nan. W a gentan konnen!*"

The syntax eluded Jacqueline, but she understood the gist of Leyla's command: *Eat, child. Eat your size stomach. This good things your darling country. You on time learn.*

Jacqueline saw that Leyla was affable and hospitable—a Haitian at heart. The woman explained that in addition to doing research as a Creolist, she worked with a grassroots organization that assisted destitute rice farmers with starting other businesses. "How can you make a living when the country is littered with cheap rice from the good old US of A?" It was then that she met the man who would become her husband, Jean-Pierre Guerrier.

Jacqueline nodded with embarrassment, feeling like she might have inadvertently made Leyla feel like she was being interrogated. "I'm an open book," Leyla said, as if she could read her prospective pupil's mind.

"When can I start gathering the lost pieces of my own language?" Jacqueline asked half-jokingly.

"Saturdays work for me," Leyla said.

"That works for me too," Jacqueline volleyed back, and they agreed on a time.

"That's it," Leyla clapped her hands, "I'll eat to that!"

Every Saturday afterward, Jacqueline went to Leyla's place for Creole lessons. Both were pleased to discover the ease with which the student's native language returned. Within weeks, pupil and teacher could hold extensive conversations in Creole.

"If you went to Haiti today, you could communicate with anyone and everyone," Leyla intoned proudly. Their conversations—banal discussions for the sake of practicing the language—soon gained more substance. Rather than staying at the café or Leyla's apartment for lessons, the two women often opted for long walks around the harbor and beyond. Once they took a bus to New York for the day, and spent hours on Nostrand Avenue, chatting in Creole with shopkeepers. Innocuous talk about the weather and politics led to meaningful conversations concerning what was always on their minds: the earthquake. Jacqueline, for her part, had stopped paying attention to the news since she spoke to Annette and learned that she and Paul had been in Florida while she had been sick with worry.

Jacqueline and Leyla talked and laughed like old friends. Here the two of them were, teacher and student, but their relationship quickly blossomed into a friendship which both desperately craved.

Speaking in Creole, Leyla explained that she and her ex-husband Jean-Pierre were married in a simple ceremony near the Artibonite River. "Shortly after the wedding, I became pregnant."

Jacqueline winked at her friend mischievously.

"Between you and me," Leyla chuckled, "that baby was conceived before the wedding night—I loved him like crazy. Jean-Pierre wanted us to move to the United States after the wedding. He'd never been here before, and was curious. He said our baby would be much safer here. I'd lived in Haiti for many, many years, and never once felt threatened. I was as safe as anybody. But as the baby grew inside of me, Jean-Pierre worried more and more. Finally,

I decided maybe coming back to the States wouldn't be so bad. We applied for a visa and got it right away. Jean-Pierre seemed happy. But I knew it was a matter of time before he would want to go back. Then, a few days before we left, I miscarried the baby."

Leyla told Jacqueline that despite what had happened, the first few weeks in America with Jean-Pierre had been blissful. He enjoyed sightseeing, gazing at the office buildings, the people, the shops—everything excited him, like a thunderstruck tourist. She took him to theme parks, where he rode roller coasters and cackled like a child. They visited the Smithsonian Museum in Washington, DC. They took selfies in Philadelphia with the Liberty Bell in the background. She took him to Madame Tussauds wax museum in Manhattan. At FAO Schwartz, he waited in line for his turn to play the floor piano with his feet. He ate seekh kabab on Avenue of the Americas. The lights of Times Square made his head spin. When they boarded a boat on the Hudson to visit the Statue of Liberty, Jean-Pierre's hands trembled with excitement—he'd never dreamed he would see Lady Liberty in person.

At home, Jean-Pierre cooked her favorite Haitian dishes. They made love constantly, and held hands when they walked. Every day was a miracle, until that morning when Leyla awoke to find Jean-Pierre gone. He had left a letter on the kitchen table, which read, *After days of fasting and intense meditation, God told me to seek another path in life. I must listen to the Lord. I am not sure where He wants me to go, but I do know He does not want me to stay here.*

Leyla remained stunned for over a year. When she finally accepted the fact that Jean-Pierre would never come back, she considered returning to Haiti, but could not imagine living there without the love of her life. That was when she decided to bring Haiti to her home in the US. She was fluent in Creole, and would teach it.

"That's more than enough about me," Leyla concluded. "Tell me about this woman who married a dashing Marine, who has a beautiful three-year old, but never talks about her family."

Jacqueline shrugged. "There's not a lot to say, really. Kevin and I met, fell in love, and got married. He served a couple of tours overseas—Afghanistan, Iraq, and who knows where else. We had Amber. I teach. He works for an engineering firm that builds vertical towns. You know, the usual stuff. Nothing spectacular."

Every Saturday after spending time with Leyla, Jacqueline returned home and took her place before the easel in her little art studio. The instant her brush touched the canvas, she was transported like an eagle sailing high above the clouds. Thousands of miles below, the ocean was a frothy lime-green. When she painted from this place above the clouds, the result was ingenious—only a master could mix colors so rich, and reduce complicated images to their most basic essence. Jacqueline hoped her work would someday find its way to an exhibit alongside those artists who inspired her so. After languishing for years in the purgatory of discouraged painters, she hoped *someday* was not an eternity away. Finishing a painting was like flying first class: the experience was restorative; transformative. When she touched down, she would be like new. Kevin would not recognize her. Amber would ask, "Mommy, is that really you?"

Jacqueline would shift on her stool—surely the flight

would end soon. The artist part of her brain would have to shut down. Reality, like a wave of impatient passengers in a crowded airplane, would rush past her. Reality did not have manners; it would not wait for her to disembark. Dinner. Laundry. Housecleaning. That reality was already rushing back. As her Saturday would draw to a close, Jacqueline would recall the carefree years when she dreamed of being a working artist, but found she could not sell enough work to make a living. The teaching job had found her, and she had accepted it. Monday through Friday her life was steeped in self-doubt, regret, and torment.

Mondays were manageable, but Tuesdays were hellish. That was when the kindergarteners flooded her classroom, demanding to become Rembrandts and Picassos. During all the years of her life, Tuesdays were always the most significant: She was born on a Tuesday. She received menarche on a Tuesday. She left her parents' house on a Tuesday. Amber was born on a Tuesday. The earthquake that pulverized much of Haiti and left her father a double amputee happened on a Tuesday.

The pile of unopened mail on the kitchen counter needed to be sorted. The empty pizza boxes needed to be put in the recycling bin. The stack of Amber's old clothes needed to be donated to the local thrift store. Kevin's slacks and jackets needed to be taken to the cleaners. His sweaters needed to be washed and folded. Reality shuffled past her. At school she would see only gray: gray walls, gray floor, gray chairs, and a gray desk. The voices of old men and women trapped in the bodies of six-year-olds would fill the gray air. She would try to ignore them, but the music teacher's harpsichord was always relentless. And the children would go on singing:

This old man, he played nine,
He played knick-knack on my vine.
With a knick-knack paddy-whack
Give a dog a bone,
This old man came rolling home . . .

Like a parolee, she was free, but not quite free enough. Saturday nights brought the realization that Sunday would come too soon. Monday would follow it, and she would need to report back to the school once used as an insane asylum for war veterans who had witnessed more in one lifetime than any human being should.

Jacqueline took solace in helping those students everyone else ignored. She thought about the sixth grader whose father had thrown the prostitute out of the bedroom window. She thought about the girl who became pregnant at twelve. The children needed her, and she would be there for them. She was ready to go back to work.

Jacqueline never called Baybrook Memorial Hospital again to try and speak to her father. During the months that followed, Annette telephoned often. "Your father thinks you hate him," she informed Jacqueline more than once. "He wants to know what he did to you to make you hate him so much."

Jacqueline did not have an answer. She programmed her phone to send calls from her mother's number directly to voice mail. She contemplated blocking the number altogether, but decided against it.

Spring and summer whizzed by; it was now nine

months since the quake had struck. Her parents had returned to the house in Haiti. Annette reported that Paul was having difficulty adjusting to his new situation, meaning his infirmity. He hated not being able to walk. He hated the stares from old friends who used to dance with him at the parties. The prostheses made it difficult to move fluidly from one place to the next. Mostly, he resented his body for failing him.

During one of Annette's lengthy phone messages, she said her husband had bought an electric wheelchair to make his life easier. But he forgot that Haiti was not one of those countries that accommodated wheelchairs. The roads were not smooth, nor did the sidewalks offer depressions for wheelchairs to cross streets.

Each time Jacqueline heard her mother's voice, she felt guilty for not calling her father. "He was lucky," Annette had said while in Miami. It didn't seem to matter to them that Jacqueline had spent weeks worrying herself sick about whether they were alive or dead. Calling him would have to wait.

SEVEN

"Jacqueline, dear, it's me." The triumph in the caller's voice infuriated her. "Your father keeps asking for you, and I worry about him. It's been close to a year since the earthquake. He goes for days without speaking to me. I came back to Haiti for him, but he's still not happy. He doesn't sleep, and when he does, he screams for his old employees to get out of the store. He relives the event every day. I don't know what to do with him. He doesn't want to leave the house. Paul prefers to shut himself inside the salon, playing one depressing song after another. He talks about you more and more. Jacqueline, if you don't come soon, who knows what might happen?"

"I can't just pick up and leave any time I want," Jacqueline responded. "I have a job and responsibilities. I don't have a babysitter for Amber, and Kevin has been working really hard on a project. He can't take time off right now. He works long hours; by the time he gets home in the evening, he's exhausted."

"It's always *Kevin this* and *Amber that*. What about your father? Doesn't he matter to you at all? Don't you care what happens to him?"

"Why don't you come visit us here, Annette? Bring Paul. There are a couple of good hotels near the harbor. You would be very comfortable here for a few days." Jacqueline regretted the words as soon as they came out of her mouth.

"Your father cannot travel," Annette said. "Besides, he's scared if he leaves Haiti for one second, the country will disappear. I doubt he'll leave ever again, as if his presence here is the only thing keeping the ground from crumbling." Before Jacqueline could speak, Annette added: "Oh, and I'm his new driver now. What kind of man lets a woman drive him around?"

Jacqueline gave no answer. The man she remembered had always refused the services of a chauffeur, even though he could have hired a dozen. She admitted to herself that she did not know him now at all. "I'll call tomorrow," she said before hanging up, knowing she would not.

EIGHT

Sundays belonged to Kevin: he was free to go anywhere and do whatever he wished. He could stay out all day with friends and come home in the middle of the night if he wanted. But there was no other friend besides Michael Baker—the former Marine with whose help Kevin acquired his supply of cure-all pills. Most days, Michael was high and sleeping it off in some stranger's bed. He went to war a happily married man and came home with divorce papers waiting for him to sign. Kevin and Michael had little in common beyond their memories of the desert; that was enough to cement their kind of friendship.

On Sundays Kevin could play video games from dawn to dawn. He could listen to all the music he wanted—with the stipulation that he wore headphones. Before the deployments, Kevin used to like Bob Marley and the Wailers, but somewhere along the way he had developed an insatiable appetite for Deicide, Meshuggah, Suffocation—bands that made Iron Maiden and Metallica sound like

Chopin or Yanni. The more guttural the singer's voice, the more unrestrained the rage and the electric guitar, the more violent and disturbing the lyrics, the more Kevin craved it. He listened with deep concentration, mouthing the words and bobbing his head as gently as he did when Amber performed her best rendition of "Under the Sea."

Kevin could become as carefree on Sundays as his wife did each Saturday. But unlike Jacqueline, who enjoyed the fantasy of being deliciously unattached, Kevin preferred spending his day with Amber. If he could quit his job and take care of his daughter full time, he would. Long before Amber was even conceived, she was the child he dreamed about during those days in Baghdad, when Death breathed on his face and defied him to have hope. This was the child—the yet-to-be-born good luck charm—who must have kept snipers' bullets from ripping into his flesh. This was the miracle baby whose freedom he fought for. She was his country now, his universe. He hated everything about war. He would never forget that nineteen-year-old boy from Ames, Iowa, who got his head blown off just one day after he arrived. He could do without ever seeing that kind of violence again, but for Amber—the light of his love—he would take up his weapon and gladly deploy to any war zone. He would die a thousand times to see his child smile the way she smiled when he read The Little Mermaid to her.

On this Sunday Jacqueline and Kevin were still in bed. He was awake, and had been since four thirty in the morning. He touched her and breathed deeply, but Jacqueline pretended to be asleep. Under the sheets, her hands curled into fists. She was tired and wanted to sleep. She planned to return to work the following day, and needed all the rest she could get before having to face her students.

Kevin prodded her in the ribs like she was his personal house girl. Jacqueline groaned angrily. "Come on, sleeping beauty. Rise and shine." Kevin kissed the back of her neck softly. Persistently.

Annoyed, Jacqueline wanted to tell him to leave her be, but knew he would sulk for days afterward. And she would feel obligated to spend a solid hour, mostly awake, speaking the only language his body understood.

"Come on," Kevin pressed, touching her with quivering fingers in places where she did not wish to be touched, particularly on a Sunday morning.

"Five more minutes," she began the slow, painful descent toward acquiescence.

Tasting his imminent victory, Kevin stretched his arms until he had his wife wrapped in them. He flipped her around to face him and forced her head to rest on his chest beneath which a riotous march played. He tickled her playfully. Jacqueline pulled the sheets over her face, wanting to disappear.

The alarm clock by Kevin's side of the bed now flashed a bright number six with two zeros behind it. Jacqueline mumbled another protest under her breath.

He prodded her again, this time more forcefully. When he tried to kiss her, she recoiled. He pulled her closer to his body, pressed his lips against her mouth. "Baby . . ." he said. She pushed him away.

Sundays belonged to Kevin. He could do anything he wanted—that was the agreement. He could have whatever he wanted, including her body.

He ran his fingers along her naked arms, and Jacqueline bristled. For a brief moment she reasoned she would let him have his way, just so he would leave her alone afterward. "I need this," he whispered, like someone dying.

"Not now," Jacqueline whispered. "My stomach hurts. Last night's dinner didn't agree with me. You don't want to come too close, trust me."

Kevin groaned. He could wait. He would wait. He had mastered the art of waiting in Fallujah, when the days were long and the nights interminable. He had learned to wait and see which of his friends would not return after a night of combat. He had learned to wait as the minutes tore into hours and hours into days.

Sanctuary. Jacqueline contemplated the word and the meaning it once held for her. If only she belonged to a church, she would have gone there before Kevin had a chance to open his eyes. There was a time when she never missed a Sunday. That was before Kevin came home from his last deployment. She never told him about the incident that made it impossible for her to return. She wondered what he would have said to her if he knew. What would he have thought of her? But the man she married never came back from the war. This Kevin was different; this Kevin was a stranger. Even the way he touched her was different. The spark that had been a fixture in her Kevin's eyes was now a black hole, threatening to swallow her. This Kevin looked like her husband, but was not the same man.

Kevin yearned to make love to his wife. Back in Fallujah, he never dared dream he would touch Jacqueline again. He had pushed those thoughts out of his mind, because love had no place in combat. Love was a mirage in the desert. The insurgents killed for love. Their victims died for love. Love was to blame for the evils of the world. Kevin wondered if love was the reason the desert floor stayed drenched with blood.

Maybe love did not actually exist. Kevin fought against this notion every time he pressed down on the accelerator on a highway, bobbing his head gently to a death metal song. Inside the car, the music would be loud enough to shatter the windows, but it was a lullaby to his ears. The screams of the band Exodus were deafening. *"War is my shepherd!"* the singer shrieked. *"You put your faith in Christianity, I put mine in artillery! My M-16, my lord and savior . . ."*

Long ago, before they were married, Jacqueline was thrilled to have him touch her, even while she slept. Her eyes would open slowly. She would reach out to him, kiss him, until they both panted with desire. She would wrap her legs around him and welcome him in the place she now kept secret. He tried to remember what it felt like to make love to her, but what he saw before his mind's eye were palm trees coated with dust, hospitals and schools pockmarked with bullet holes, bodies frozen in the fetal position from the effects of mustard gas. No one had told him there would be so many palm trees in a war zone.

He had Jacqueline within reach now, but she was not the same person he once knew either. Her chest rose and fell like the woman he married, but the heart inside no longer beat for him. Sometimes he felt as if she wanted him gone. Perhaps she had spent so much time alone when he was away that she no longer needed or wanted him. But going to war was a decision that had been made for him—it had not been his choice to engage in battle with people whose names he never even knew. That Kevin belonged in another man's skin. But here he was, carrying the residue of disaster with him morning, noon, and night. Here he was, resented by his own wife for what he did not mean to do.

The urge to be inside of her was unbearable. He nuzzled her face with the tip of his nose, tracing her collarbone with unsure fingers.

Jacqueline spoke through gritted teeth: "Leave me alone, Kevin."

He retracted. He understood the words. He knew what it meant to want to be left alone.

"Leave me alone," she repeated, this time with a cruel tone. Him. Kevin. Her husband. The man who would have died for her a thousand times. He wondered if she would have wanted him to leave her alone in that place where snipers seldom missed their targets. Would she have screamed in horror if she had seen his feet blistered from wearing boots in the infernal heat? Would she have fled if she'd seen his back covered with scabs, his face layered with dust, his uniform stiff with caked blood? She had wanted him to come home then. She said so every time they talked. She wanted him alive. Nothing else mattered. And here he was now, alive, but that did not seem to matter.

Between deployments, their love had been stronger than before. They sent each other the sort of text messages they could view only in private places. Now, Jacqueline shrank each time he came near. They slept in the same bed, but worlds apart. In the mornings, if they caught each other's eyes by accident, they saw only despair.

The wounded look on Kevin's face made her wish *she* was

the one who had gone to war. She could have handled it. She wouldn't have fallen apart afterward. She was a Florestant—Annette Florestant's daughter. She would have returned unscathed. And she would not beg a man to touch her on a peaceful Sunday morning. As a matter of fact, she would get up, go for a nice walk, come back, and take advantage of the morning light to work on a painting. Moments like these made Jacqueline wish she was still single. She would be free. The entire week would belong to her. She could do whatever she chose, not just on Saturdays.

Maybe Kevin was right: girls who spent quality time with their fathers did not rush into marriage.

Kevin turned away, mumbling expletives under his breath.

NINE

"I can talk all day long, but you're the one taking language lessons," Leyla snarled facetiously. "You're supposed to talk more than I do! This learning method is easy. We have conversations; we discuss any subject you choose."

"That's the craziest method I've ever heard."

"We could always conjugate verbs and learn vocabulary out of context, but how effective would that be?" Leyla countered. "And don't forget, you're the one who didn't want to go the *conventional route*. Remember telling me that?"

"Yes, I do."

"Tell me your darkest secret in Creole. I can listen as a therapist, correct you like a teacher, and answer like a friend. This way we feed three birds with one seed. I've told you so much about myself, now it's your turn."

"I know."

"You can think of this as an exam, if that'll make you talk to me."

"Ha! I didn't think I was paying you for exams."

"You're not paying me at all," Leyla reminded her. "I told you a long time ago that your money isn't good here."

"Fine." Jacqueline took a long breath. "You know how Saturdays are mine and Kevin gets Sundays?"

"The cutest little arrangement I've ever heard, if you ask me."

"It wasn't always that way. I used to have Sundays too."

Leyla feigned shock. "Dear God, what happened to make you give up the Sabbath?" Her eyes were not as disarming as they had been when Jacqueline saw them for the first time. In fact, the vivid blue was now gentle and welcoming, lighting the way into Leyla's kind heart. Jacqueline felt as if she had known her all her life. Did she love her?

The old Jacqueline took comfort in the sanctuary when Kevin was overseas. Now, when she thought of church, all she saw before her was her former preacher with that tortured look on his face, asking the congregation for time to "rethink" his calling. Translation: his mistress's belly had swollen beyond any lie the usually loquacious pastor could tell. His wife, the first lady, was so incensed she shared the news with anyone who had ears to hear. The first lady's unabashed ownership of the scandal won her so many points with the elders that they left it up to her to wash away the stain from the church's otherwise stellar reputation. The ostrich plume in her hat had quivered when she informed her husband—moments before he was due to preach—that someone else would be delivering the sermon. The church held its breath that morning, watching apprehensively.

Tears spurted out of the pastor's eyes as he offered his flock a plethora of justifications for having made the choices that led to his predicament. "The demonic spirit of fornication slithered into my life," he said in a trembling voice. "Brothers and sisters, beware! The principalities are still at large, and coiled like snakes under somebody's pew as sure as I stand here before you. I fought a good fight against the devil and succumbed. I knew I was being used by the Almighty as an instrument to bring this congregation closer to salvation; for this reason, I accepted my fall. The Lord used me and my weakness to be an example to you, brothers and sisters. My flesh refuses to accept my sin, but my soul knows its transgressions. God has forgiven me. Now it's your turn to forgive. I know you will do the godly thing and give your pastor another chance."

His wife kept her eyes on the congregation, which stood and applauded wildly. The pastor kept his head bowed in humility.

The interim pastor, Sister Marsha, checked her watch and cleared her throat loudly in the microphone. Once she had everyone's attention, she made a sweeping motion with her hands. This was her pulpit now—her stage, her mountaintop. Men, women, and children stared forward, eagerly anticipating the word that would come forth from this woman of God. Sunrays fell in slants across Sister Marsha's face. The effect transformed her into one of those tigers which Jacqueline taught the students to draw at school.

Sister Marsha cocked her head and shimmied her shoulders. With the same steady hands that she had used to calm the congregation, she signaled a couple of large but pious-looking men to escort the disgraced pastor out of view. The former first lady sat in her regular prominent seat. This would be her last time there, and she wanted to experience the moment without having to share the spotlight with her deceitful husband.

Sister Marsha shimmied her shoulders again—this would become a trademark move—and settled into her new role like yolk inside an egg. After a few unintelligible words in a strange tongue, she spoke words that everyone in the church understood. She chided the congregation for the generous applause they had lavished on the former pastor. Didn't they know it was wrong—if not unforgivable—to break God's most explicit rule about the sanctity of marriage? Trading one's wife of twenty-seven years for a groupie was bad enough. Getting her pregnant was so mind-boggling that decades of torment would be too light a sentence, and hell too remote a location, for the sinner's rebuke to serve the greater good. The former pastor's punishment needed to be witnessed by every man, particularly the married kind.

Sister Marsha went on about the perils of extramarital sex, premarital sex, homosexual sex, and bestiality. She told everyone listening that only ardent prayer and total abstinence would deliver them from such urges.

"I was once like you," she informed the congregation. "Before I was saved, I too was in the world. Don't think I'm so sanctified that I don't know what's what. I know what you do, because I was one of you. I was not always saintly and without stain. But you see, I brought my worldliness, my sins, and my stains before the Lord— and He made me clean. He pulled me out of the ditch and baptized me with fire, amen."

The congregation responded, "Yes, tell it, Pastor! Preach it!"

She went on: "I was raped at fourteen years of age by an uncle. As a result of that violence, a child was born from me. The man who raped me went on to attack dozens of other girls. All because I kept his secret. I did not tell, I kept the darkness inside of me. And I kept the child—a boy. Many years later, when someone found the courage to expose this demon, and so many other girls came forward to tell the secrets they had kept, I added my voice to theirs. I emptied myself of the darkness, and I gave my life to Christ right then and there, and never looked back. I vowed I would become a voice, a loud voice, for those who can't or are too scared to speak for themselves. Mouths don't speak, they say, but I refuse to keep the secrets of evildoers! I will not placate them with silence. Silence is a tool of the enemy who does nothing but lie all day long, amen. The word says, *Let everything that hath breath, praise ye the Lord.* So I shall praise Him until I breathe my last. The word also tells us that *every head shall bow, every tongue confess that He alone is God.* So I stopped by to let you know that I shall bow my head and confess that there is no greater God than the Great I Am. Are you with me?" She raised her finger toward the ceiling. "Last I checked, God is still on the throne. I don't care what car you drive. I don't care what all the diplomas on your office walls say about you. I don't care how many members you have in your church—you are not God, you are not holy. You are a small-minded reptile. And therefore you cannot lead a congregation such as this."

The crowd shouted in agreement. Some slapped each other's shoulders. They raised their hands heavenward, threw their heads back, and shouted, "Amen!"

Sister Marsha was unstoppable. The church members loved her instantly. She knew it, and in her heart, she loved them too. She wanted to wrap her arms around them, comfort them, and explain to them that the best was still yet to come. "I know a few ministers have looked the other way in this church, when they should have been leading you to righteousness. If you will let *this* pastor lead," she pounded her chest, "if you will allow me to guide you, this church will see a revival like no other. If anyone under the sound of my voice has a problem with the word of God, pick up your Bible and leave now." Eyes swiveled. Some of the congregants considered walking out, but feared the reproachful looks and whispers that would greet them at the neighborhood grocery store and their children's schools and parks. "Get thee behind me!" Sister Marsha roared. "Get out of this church or bow down before the one God there is and ever will be!"

While the sun continued to throw its blinding light across Sister Marsha's animated face, and she continued to shimmy her shoulders, the soft skin underneath Jacqueline's eyes twitched. She fixed her gaze on the hymn book in the wooden box attached to the pew in front of her. While Sister Marsha went on raging about sex and other sins, Jacqueline swallowed the bile forcing its way up her throat, keeping her eye on the pastor. For a moment, everything was a blur. The air was thick, and she could see nothing.

When she was able to focus again, a throng of people were staring down at her, pinning her to the floor with their strong arms and hands. Jacqueline wondered if she had suffered a seizure. She'd never had seizures in the past, but life being life, anything was possible.

"Are you okay?" Sister Marsha asked. She placed a hand on Jacqueline's forehead as if to take her temperature. "She doesn't have a fever."

"She's out of her mind!" someone shrieked angrily.

"She wicked like all them Haitians. Got the devil in her sure as I'm standing here. We oughta call the police and let them deal with her."

Sister Marsha's voice was soothing and maternal: "This is more proof that the devil will try every trick in the book to keep me from leading this congregation toward the path of rectitude. I am more convinced of that now, but I shall not be moved. I said it before and I'll say it again: Get thee behind me, Satan."

Someone slapped Jacqueline hard across the face. "Wake up, you demon!"

She opened her eyes with a start. A drop of blood trickled from Sister Marsha's lip and fell on Jacqueline's forehead. "Do you need a ride home, my child?" the pastor asked.

"She just fine!" someone else bellowed. "She just crazy is all. How you gonna throw a hymnal at your own pastor? We don't need her kind in here, no how. I vote for getting her arrested for assault and battery. We got plenty of witnesses to testify as to what happened here."

Jacqueline struggled to stand. "What happened?" she asked, reaching for her purse.

"She act like she don't even know what she did. Don't believe her, Sister Marsha. She lyin just like all them witches from Hay-dees."

"That would be *Hay-ee-tee*," Sister Marsha corrected the speaker, the way a teacher might. She now held a handkerchief to her upper lip. "But God as my witness, we will pray the devil right out of this church." The pastor took Jacqueline's hand and helped her to her feet. "Ain't nothing wrong with you, sweetheart. Don't ever think there is." She walked with Jacqueline toward the exit. "You okay going home, my dear?"

"Yes," Jacqueline said, and teetered to her car.

When Jacqueline returned to the church many weeks later to apologize, Sister Marsha wrapped her arms around her. "I know you did not mean to do what you did. As far as I'm concerned, you were being used by the enemy to try and deter me, but I passed that test, amen. I prayed about it, and I prayed for you."

Ashamed, Jacqueline could not stop apologizing. The more she looked at Sister Marsha, however, the more she noticed that it was Annette she was seeing before her. The resemblance was uncanny.

"This is your house of worship," Sister Marsha said. "I expect to see you next Sunday bright and early."

Jacqueline had walked out of the church and planned never to return. "I haven't been back since," she now told Leyla. She cringed at the memory of what she had done.

"That's quite a story," Leyla said, taking Jacqueline's face in her hands. She peered deep into her friend's eyes. "Everyone has at least one little secret. Yours is really not that scandalous, so I recommend two Hail Marys and some dancing." A smile played on Leyla's lips.

"What?"

Leyla picked up her phone and turned the volume as high as it would go. A singer with a powerful voice sang an upbeat song in Creole. "You need a little music in your life." She took Jacqueline's hands, shaking them as if there were a hundred leeches attached to her skin. Leyla sang along, raising her voice high to match the furious beat. She let go of Jacqueline's hands and bent her knees slightly, as if to curtsy in supplication. From that position, her shoulders and arms undulated up and down slowly, gracefully, in a serpentine fashion. "Do you know how to dance the Yanvalou?" Leyla asked, raising and lowering her head, arching the length of her back. It looked as if she did not have a spinal column.

"I'm not in a dancing mood," Jacqueline said in a semi-agitated voice, not wanting to embarrass herself.

"I'm not in a dancing mood either. But this music will make up your mind for you." Drums overtook the space: riotous, infectious. Leyla motioned for her friend to surrender.

Jacqueline stood as rigidly as a light post. She remembered Pachou playing similar music when she was a child, and feeling herself wanting to dance. Annette had been so incensed she had threatened to throw Pachou out. "This sounds a lot like voodoo music to me," Jacqueline scoffed. "And just because I'm Haitian doesn't mean I'm into that stuff."

Leyla stopped dancing and threw her hands in the air. "What people call *voodoo* is the crap somebody made up to sell movie tickets. Besides, Foula's music is called vodou jazz. The messages are mostly political, not religious. As a matter of fact, the band had to go into hiding to keep from getting killed. The bass player, Chico Boyer, is one of the top musicians in the world. I saw them play a couple of times, the crowd could not get enough."

"I know what vodou jazz is," Jacqueline snapped. "Don't assume that there's some planet where you could pass for being more Haitian than I am."

"Of course," Leyla replied.

"Gotta go," Jacqueline said abruptly, and rushed out.

When Jacqueline fetched her mail three days later, she found a Foula CD in the pile—Leyla knew her better than she thought. She tore open the shrink wrap and played the CD, undulating her arms and shoulders the way Leyla had done. The difference was that Jacqueline's movements were even more fluid, and came from a place so deep within her that it was as if she had danced the Yanvalou every day of her life. She moved as if she did not have a bone in her body. Her arms, back, hips, legs: every part of her was pliable.

Over the next week, when Jacqueline played the CD, she would take Kevin by the hand and spin him around the kitchen island as if it were a grand ballroom. He dreaded those moments, saying they made him feel odd. But that would not stop him from wanting to lead.

"The man is supposed to lead," Kevin said when they danced together. She would let him for a minute or two, then with one deft move and a twist of her hip, she would usurp him. He would stop and swat the air with annoyance. The fact was, as Jacqueline later told Leyla, the man danced like both feet were in one muddy boot.

If she could not dance with Amber or Kevin, Jacqueline would dance alone. There, in the middle of their kitchen, when Kevin was not home, she danced to the drums. How many times did Kevin catch her twirling around with one hand on her heart and the other in the air? He would be partly amused and partly vexed. One evening he asked, "Since when did you become so addicted to that voodoo music?"

"It's called vodou jazz," Jacqueline said. "Leyla told me about this band, Foula. I like their music a lot, it reminds me of Haiti. You could say I'm dancing with the memories."

"What memories are those?" Kevin asked with a hint of condescension.

Jacqueline did not respond.

"Oh, yes. You must remember the times you drank milk out of the baby bottle. And yes, you had pigtails and rode in a chauffeur-driven car to school. Don't forget the one where Annette and Paul let you down every chance they get, starting from the day you turned ten years old and they dumped you in a faraway country just so they could be free."

Jacqueline bit down on a response, but Kevin's words had cut to the bone. She escaped to her studio to contemplate an unfinished painting on the easel before her. She closed her eyes and wondered what on earth had convinced her she could paint any better than a five-year-old. Frustration tore through her. She gritted her teeth angrily and fought against the urge to drive a knife through the canvas. An incoming call gave her a needed reprieve. The familiar voice on the other end did not annoy her this time.

"*Alo*, Annette! *Sak pase?*"

"It's your father," Annette began. "Things aren't well at all. You know he's always had a weak constitution. I tell him we need to get out of this place, but he won't hear any of it. We could move to Palm Beach or Long Island. Hell, I'd be willing to move to Osaka, Japan, for all I care. You have to come as soon as you can, Jacqueline, or you might never see him again."

Jacqueline listened with the usual skepticism. Something more was going on than what her mother was saying, and she wondered what it might be. Even though Paul and Annette were her parents, she did not really know them. Right then she remembered the lavish parties they threw, and the adoration in their guests' faces, but nothing more.

TEN

"We have to talk," Jacqueline said, touching Kevin's arm.

He stiffened. "What about?"

"We need to go to Haiti."

"What for?"

"I have to see Paul. According to Annette, he's not doing well at all."

"Since when do you believe anything that comes out of your mother's beak?"

"It's been over a year since the earthquake. He was severely injured, and I have yet to speak a full sentence to him."

"No thanks. I deployed to Haiti when that president almost got the shit kicked out of him. No offense, but if I never see that country again, I'll be fine."

"We don't have a choice," Jacqueline said. "And I want you to come with us."

"Who's *us*?"

"Us. Me, Amber."

Kevin cleared his throat. "Not in this lifetime; Amber will never set foot in that place."

"You ought to know that Haiti is not half the hellhole people think it is. Besides, our family could use this time together."

"Our family?"

"Whether or not we like it, Kevin, Paul and Annette Florestant are a part of *our* family."

"I'm not the one who needs reminding," Kevin barked.

"Annette called twice yesterday."

"Impressive!"

"She said Paul won't eat. He stays in bed most days and cries like a child."

"Surprise, surprise! Miss Melodrama Universe takes the crown for the twenty-fifth consecutive year."

"My father almost died." Jacqueline's body shivered as she uttered the words. For years she'd thought her parents were invincible. Immortal. She recalled watching with awe as a child when they drove through life at full speed, never slowing down—not even at the sharpest turns.

"Both of your parents will outlive us." Kevin, the engineer, apparently doubled as a fortune-teller.

"Annette said she doesn't know how much longer he'll live." Jacqueline tried to keep her voice free of the frustration churning inside. "She asked if we were waiting for one of them to die before we visit."

"Your mother has a PhD in manipulation," Kevin snarled.

"We haven't seen them since Amber's baptism."

"They could have come to Amber's birthdays, or Christmases, but I guess they had more important business. What's another four years?" Kevin shrugged.

"Amber is their only grandchild, and I'm their only child."

"Got news for you, Jackie: you're no longer a child. And besides, the State Department says to steer clear of Haiti unless you've got urgent business down there."

"My father almost died," Jacqueline said sharply. "Is visiting him urgent enough business?"

"Depends on whom you ask."

"It wouldn't hurt the artist in me to get a quick refresher course, you know. Colors are fading in my mind. My landscapes are half dead."

"If you're looking for inspiration, google it. Get on YouTube and watch a couple news reports from those channels that wouldn't dream of leaving out the gory stuff. You can restock your mental supply room without having to step on a minefield."

"I didn't expect you to understand," Jacqueline said. She recalled the school principal telling her—with conceit—how effortlessly he negotiated the known world via Google.

"I do understand. The State Department does too."

"I don't care what the State Department says about my country!"

"Haiti hasn't been your country for twenty-five years. Get real." Kevin waited for a reaction, but Jacqueline preferred to swallow her own tongue than let him think his words held any power.

Suddenly Amber ran into their bedroom with both arms in the air, like a tiny soldier surrendering. Jacqueline scooped her up.

"Four years, Kevin. That's how long it's been since Annette and Paul have seen their grandchild."

Kevin's eyes softened. "Tell your devoted *manman* to meet us in Miami. We'll have dinner at that Haitian restaurant in South Beach. We'll kiss hello on one cheek and goodbye on the other."

Jacqueline's eyes twitched. She was dangerously close to hitting that emergency red button inside her head.

Leaning on the bedroom wall now, Kevin searched his wife's eyes. "It's all those Creole lessons with Leyla, isn't it? You're ready to practice on real Haitians." He laughed contemptuously.

"I've already bought the tickets," Jacqueline confessed.

"Seriously?" He pounded his chest and coughed as if he had swallowed a lump of food without chewing it. Jacqueline's eyes roamed over his chest. Kevin was lean and defined, his skin smooth—he was beautiful. Jacqueline wondered why she no longer desired him the way she once had.

She said, "We never go anywhere. You must have years' worth of vacation time piled up at work. As for me, God knows I need a break. Those kids and their grown-up stories are killing me. I need to reassess before next school year hits me like a rocket."

"Shit!"

Jacqueline covered Amber's ears with her hands. "Do you have to talk like that in front of our child?"

"Do you have to make these big decisions without telling me?"

"Visiting my parents hardly falls in the 'big decisions' category." Jacqueline's voice bounced off the walls and settled like black fog between them.

"It does if your parents live in a fucking war zone."

"Daddy, what's *fucking*?" Amber inquired dreamily.

"Something little girls shouldn't say," Kevin replied.

"You can't believe everything you hear," Jacqueline murmured.

She wanted to introduce Kevin to the part of her he had never seen. She wanted to remember the person she was long ago, before leaving Haiti. The country was a part of her no matter how much she tried to run away from it. Now that she was learning Creole again, she felt an urge to return, even if it was just for a few days. "Kevin, please, come with us."

"Not on your life."

"*Pa gen pwoblèm*," she said, secretly thanking Leyla for giving her the old language back. "We'll go without you!" she blasted. "*M pral fout ale san ou. Ki mele m?*"

Jacqueline was curious about all the Build Haiti Back Better progress the journalists raved about. She wanted to see with her own eyes what the nonprofit organizations had done with the money they collected after the quake. She could not recall how much she herself had sent, but it was plenty.

Kevin stormed into the bathroom, mumbling angrily in Pashto. She yelled back in Creole, wielding her mother tongue like an old knife, freshly sharpened and polished to look and slice like new. Soon she would take Amber to Leyla's for Creole lessons, but for now the language belonged to her alone.

"Are you mad at Daddy?" Amber wanted to know.

"Never."

"Why is Daddy sad?"

"Daddy is not sad, Sunshine." Jacqueline gave a quick and nervous smile. "When he comes out of the shower, we'll tickle him until he starts to laugh so much that tears come out of his eyes, okay?"

"Okay, Mommy."

Kevin returned to the bedroom minutes later with a towel cinched around his waist. Jacqueline could not discern if there were tears caught in his eyelashes or droplets of water.

"I worry about you," he volunteered in an uncharacteristically frail voice.

"No one here is being deployed to Haiti," Jacqueline said. "My father almost died in the earthquake. I should have visited him last year, but I didn't, and he's getting old. I am not exactly looking forward to the trip, but I have to see him. Plus, Annette said he's not doing well at all."

"I don't care what that woman said. She's manipulative and a liar."

"People change."

"Look, Jackie, you don't like what I'm saying, but you know it's the truth. Going to Haiti is a bad idea, especially now. I don't have a good feeling about this."

"*Chéri* . . ." He liked it when she called him that. The corners of his mouth curled upward slightly, but his eyes remained murky. "You haven't had a good feeling about anything since you came home from the desert." Jacqueline immediately wished she had kept that thought to herself, but she was tired of treating a grown man—a Marine—like antique lace. She knew better than anyone how fragile life was. Kevin had witnessed more than any human being ought to in one lifetime. He was emotionally fractured; she understood that. "Why can't you understand why I have to go?"

"It's not a good idea," Kevin answered.

Jacqueline swallowed the bitter retort that rose to her throat. She fixed her eyes on Kevin, but said nothing. She knew her mother was adept at exaggerating stories, but she would not have lied about Paul's near-death accident. It had been over a year since she sat in her living room watching the platinum-haired anchorman repeat over and over again how resilient the Haitian people were. She recalled holding the cell phone to her chest, hoping for news about the family she hadn't seen for years. One moment she felt like she owed them a visit; the next, she wanted to curse them for letting her go on thinking they had been crushed to death under a heap of rubble. Paul and Annette Florestant were fortunate. Their kind was always fortunate. Yes, she would visit them—at least for a little while. Yes, she would go back to Haiti. She had Amber and Creole. And hopefully Leyla.

Jacqueline knew all she needed to do was ask, and Leyla would join her. She texted the words: *Come to Haiti with me*.

And Leyla responded: *Thought you'd never ask. LOL.*

When Jacqueline forwarded her itinerary, Leyla tried desperately to get that same flight. *Flight's full*, she texted. She managed to secure the last empty seat on a flight leaving the day after Jacqueline would arrive. *Can't wait*, Leyla sent.

Ditto! Jacqueline replied, and sighed before shutting off her phone.

ELEVEN

No one who knew Annette Florestant would ever accuse her of being superstitious. She ate *tourtiere* on Good Friday, and preferred the lamb version. When she saw a rainbow, she pointed, called it by name, and still did not expect to lose her finger. Annette did not like black butterflies—not because she believed they were bad omens, she simply thought they were ugly. But just in case there was some truth to the old wives' tales, she did wear a black bra and matching panties under her blindingly white wedding dress. Annette's father had outlived her mother, and she was determined not to meet a similar fate.

No one who knew Annette would have guessed she had followed the ancient tradition of burying Jacqueline's afterbirth underneath the oldest and strongest breadfruit tree on the property. Her newborn's umbilical stump took root, and the tree now stood as the tallest on the property.

Kevin was not rooted to any part of the United States the way Jacqueline was to Haiti. His own umbilical cord was who-knew-where. His family had moved to a different city every time a bird chirped.

Kevin didn't like to talk about his childhood, and it made him nervous now when people remarked that he and his father could have passed for twins—if the elder

Marshall were still alive. They had identical tempera-
ments too, which explained why Kevin despised Haiti. He
was the type of man who needed everything in life to line
up and face one direction, like the shirts in his closet. He
preferred his socks folded together, not rolled into mis-
shapen balls. He followed schedules to the second without deviating. He thrived on life's rotation of predictable
cycles. How would he know what to do in a place everyone agreed was the very definition of chaos? He had
known since he was a boy that he would become an engineer. The military was a way to offset college costs, not
engage strangers in combat.

When he returned home after his third and last tour,
Jacqueline credited her faith in God for saving Kevin's
life. How else could she have explained it? Thousands did
not make it back home alive. But he did—without a single
visible scar.

Within weeks after his return, Kevin found work at a
prestigious engineering firm that specialized in supply-
ing the ever-increasing demand for colossal office com-
pounds, upscale shopping malls, and vertical villages to
accommodate the influx of highly educated residents flee-
ing suburbia for city living. The more complex the building project, the more Kevin enjoyed it. He was an early
riser and an insomniac, a lethal combination for someone whose mind could never shut down. The few hours
of sleep allotted to him each night were spent mostly in
foreign lands—the desert, places where the inhabitants
spoke languages that sounded like secret codes.

Early in their marriage, his favorite girl was Jacqueline. Once Amber came, Kevin's loyalty shifted, and his
love for his daughter consumed him. Jacqueline reveled in

knowing that should fate treat her roughly, Kevin would take care of their daughter. He would make sure that she grew up in a safe environment. She took comfort in knowing that Kevin would kill or give his own life for his child.

Each job assignment he accepted had two non-negotiable stipulations: he would not travel out of state, and he needed to leave the site before dark every night. What he did not tell his employers was that his was the last face he wanted Amber to see before she went to sleep.

Months after returning from the blood-soaked theater with its bullet-riddled stage, Kevin appeared to be his usual self. He said nothing of the flesh-and-blood figures frozen in grotesque poses from inhaling the poisoned air supplied in abundance, all in the name of love. Kevin never discussed the date palm trees decapitated by artillery, leaving nothing more than the memory of a long-ago time when businessmen strolled avenues of self-indulgence, eel-skin briefcases in hand, and ladies—blanketed from head to feet in black—shopped for designer jeans and lace-trimmed lingerie.

Kevin never discussed what happened in the desert. The few times when Jacqueline asked, he met her gaze with stares so cold she dropped the subject. She read all she could about the transitioning process of combat veterans to civilian life. The first thing she learned was that nothing would ever be the same again. There would be no such thing as going home again for war veterans.

The only trouble was that Kevin would never ask for help. "I'm cool," he always said. They could be at a party with friends, and Kevin would sequester himself in a dark, empty room; or he'd go outside to sit alone. People made him nervous. A dog barking unhinged him. He could hear someone's footsteps from a mile away. He was always alert, always ready to defend himself against the enemies no one but he could see—like the stranger who sometimes knocked on their apartment door at night.

"We'll have a nice time," Jacqueline persisted. "Haiti is not the desert."

"Not interested."

"My parents' house is safe, I promise."

"The world is full of desperate people, Jackie. Desperate people are crazy. Haiti is full of desperate people. I've had my share of crazy. I don't want you there, and I do not want my daughter there."

"Haiti is not at war," Jacqueline said, growing annoyed.

"But it is unstable," Kevin shot back. "Any country where someone can march into the national palace and declare himself president is not safe. Shoot me if I'm wrong for not wanting my wife and child there."

"I've told you already that we'll be at my parents' house. Their place is safer than the palace."

"Your national palace crumbled like old cake over a year ago, remember?"

Jacqueline pretended not to hear. "I'm serious. My parents' house is like a fort and a spa combined. We could swim in the pool and eat fruit straight from the trees all day long. We would not have to lift a finger. It would be like a second honeymoon—doesn't that sound good?"

Kevin wouldn't budge.

"Come on, honey. I promise not to take to the streets with a group of machete-wielding demonstrators. Amber and I won't start our own political party or initiate a coup d'état."

Kevin grinned, and Jacqueline wondered if she was finally getting through to him. They would rediscover each other. The sultry moonlit nights and the carefree days in the pool would heal their marital wounds. Their lips and their eyes might find each other again.

As if he could read Jacqueline's thoughts, Kevin said: "My answer is still no."

Amber's eyes oscillated between her parents. It was Jacqueline who broke the silence, saying, "Too bad Daddy will miss all the fun."

Anger burned in Kevin's eyes. Jacqueline smiled, knowing Leyla would be with her. She would take his place.

In bed that night, silence covered them like an old, wet, musty wool blanket. Kevin had taken his pill, determined to sleep as deeply as he could and still wake up in the morning, but sleep eluded him.

As Jacqueline's own eyelids grew heavier, she heard the faint sound of Kevin sobbing. She reached over and placed her arm across his back. In one quick move, he pinned her facedown. He straddled her, and held one of her arms behind her.

"Who the hell are you?" he roared.

As she had done numerous times before, Jacqueline used her free hand to reach under her pillow for her own weapon. The photograph showed a beautiful bride dressed in a long white sheath dress. Drop earrings framed her face. The veil had been lifted at the ceremony hours before. And now she and Kevin posed for the first time as man and wife. He stood closely behind her, his arms around her waist, so that both of them appeared to be holding the bouquet of calla lilies.

Had it taken a few seconds longer for Kevin to realize that the person pinned between his powerful thighs was his wife, she might have died. They held each other afterward, knowing their lives would never be the same.

The next morning, as soon as the alarm clock went off, Kevin slipped a hand between the mattress and the box spring. He removed the hunting knife that had replaced the gun under his side of the bed. He promised Jacqueline he would see a doctor who specialized in detangling a man's good angel from his horned twin—the one who talked to him all the time, leaving him messages as if his head were an answering machine. Twice on his way home from work, the horned twin had told Kevin to park the car and jump off the Bay Bridge. "You'll thank me. Trust me."

The alarm clock next to his side of the bed was a prop, as Kevin did not need it to wake up. Back in the desert, he could stay awake for days without blinking. Jacqueline didn't mind the clock. It was not as threatening as the serrated edges that could shred her in seconds. Even so, she continued to keep her own weapon under her pillow. The wedding picture was not even printed on quality paper, but it was proof that she was his wife and not the enemy. *See, honey, see?*

 TWELVE

Six days remained before Kevin and Jacqueline would have to face the inevitable. During the first seventy-two hours, Jacqueline touched him seductively, as she had not done in years. He held her as tightly as he could without squeezing the breath out of her. He covered the length of her body with lingering kisses. They indulged in the kind of lovemaking they had perfected before Kevin's three tours, believing each time could be their last.

They laughed the way they used to before he flew to the deadly desert. They laughed at his fear of visiting Haiti. They laughed at the dangers of the world—perceived and otherwise. In the mornings they ate breakfast together, a ritual that had ended long ago. They huddled close together, singing "Under the Sea."

The evening before their departure, Amber opened her arms as far apart as they could go. "I love you *this* much," she said. The words left her parents breathless.

Jacqueline's heart swelled with hope: he would come to Haiti with them. He would protect her against those little poison darts shooting out of Annette's mouth. Leyla would be there too, and everything would be perfect. But at dinner, she pretended not to notice how slowly and painfully he chewed his food. His eyes were angry slits.

"We're leaving in the morning," she said. "You can still join us if you wish."

He kept on chewing slowly, too slowly. He did not respond.

"Will you at least drive us to the airport in the morning?"

"Can't do that," he said, staring at his plate. "I have an early meeting."

"Since when do you have to be at work at three thirty in the morning?"

He shrugged his shoulders.

"We'll take a cab," Jacqueline said.

At precisely 3:30 the following morning, the taxi announced its arrival with an explosion from its horn. Kevin held Amber in his arms, not wanting to let go.

"Why can't Daddy come with us?"

"Yes, Daddy, why can't you come with us?" Jacqueline asked in a child's voice. "There's still time. It won't take you more than five minutes to throw a few things in a bag and come with us. You served your country very well. I am sure the airline would welcome this opportunity to let you ride in their little plane for a couple of hours." Her voice rang with a mixture of desperation and sarcasm.

Kevin addressed Amber: "Daddy has to work, but I'll see you in a few days. When you come back, we'll get the biggest ice cream cone in the world, with lots of sprinkles on it."

"Ice cream with lots of sprinkles!" Amber giggled.

"How about Mommy?" Jacqueline murmured. "What will I get?"

"Mommy is a grown woman who needs to make up her mind about what she wants," Kevin said. "Let's hope, for

Mommy's sake, she makes up her mind soon." He made sure Amber faced away from Jacqueline, then mouthed the words, *Fuck you*.

"Let's go," Jacqueline said. When she reached for Amber, Kevin opened the door and went out into the hallway. The door swung closed before Jacqueline had a chance to go through, nearly smashing her face.

She toted her small suitcase and the booster seat. When she reached the taxi, she secured the booster in the backseat. After several more kisses, Kevin placed Amber in the seat. He tugged the harness across his daughter's small chest, making sure all the points were secure.

"Say bye-bye to Daddy," Jacqueline said, shutting the car door.

"Bye-bye, Daddy." Amber wanted Kevin to come sit in the car with her, but all he did was push his head through the open window to kiss her. The child reached with both arms, taking his face in her small hands.

"I'm going to miss my girl," he said somberly, and planted a kiss on her nose.

Jacqueline whispered, "See you in a week," but Kevin ignored her. "I'll bring you something nice," she added, and blew an air kiss. He spat on the ground.

The cab driver revved the engine, letting them know he'd had enough of the drawn-out goodbye scene. Kevin moved aside. Within seconds, his family was gone.

THIRTEEN

At Toussaint Louverture Airport in Port-au-Prince, Annette checked her watch and studied the board of arrivals and departures. "She'll be here soon," she said to her husband for what had to have been the hundredth time. Annette sighed dramatically. She ran her fingers along her pearl necklace. She was not accustomed to waiting.

Paul nodded. The look of patience and calm covered his frustration well. The back of his neck was wet with sweat. He wanted to bolt out of the airport and find his comfortable chair on the shaded porch or in the air-conditioned salon. The prostheses fit well enough, but he hated to wear them; they made him itch. He loathed the lopsided limp which he was certain made him look as fragile and vulnerable as a sapling in a cyclone.

As the plane prepared to land, Amber pawed at her ears and whimpered. Her eyes were flooded with tears. "Let's play the swallow game," Jacqueline said. "Close your eyes and swallow as hard as you can." Amber swallowed a couple of times, then rested her head on her mother's chest. Jacqueline made small, gentle circles on Amber's back. The earache slowly subsided.

As soon as the plane touched the tarmac, passengers unbuckled their seat belts, leaped out of their seats, and began unlatching the overhead cabinets full of carry-on luggage. They acted as if one more minute onboard would have killed them. They could not wait to set foot on Haitian soil, contrary to all the warnings from various sources.

When it was her turn to exit the plane, Jacqueline felt her throat close around a hard lump. Her head ached and her hands were moist. She remembered Kevin's words: *Haiti is always at war. Haiti is always in chaos* . . . In spite of her husband's cruelty, she wished he had accompanied her— her man, her hero, her Marine, with his undeniably good looks. The presence of her own personal soldier would let prospective criminals know that touching a single hair on her head would shorten their lives.

Jacqueline secured one of Amber's hands in hers as they made their way down the escalator. At the entrance to immigration, a troubadour band welcomed visitors with acoustic guitars, maracas, and a sweet-voiced singer who carried on about Mother Haiti. The heat was stifling. Amber reached up with her free hand, wanting to be carried. Jacqueline hoisted her up to her chest, holding her protectively.

She hated Kevin for not coming with them. He would have helped her carry Amber, the booster seat, and her luggage. It was awkward and challenging, but she would manage. She could hear his voice in her head warning her about chaos and kidnappings, killings and violent coups d'états. She could do without his pessimism for a few days. Leyla would come the next day, and they would enjoy themselves in her own private Haiti.

Didn't he understand that danger was omnipresent? Living was a dangerous undertaking. He could have died a thousand deaths in the infernal desert, but he didn't. The light fixture above the dining table could have collapsed on their heads any number of times during dinner. She could have died in the taxi on the way to the airport. Kevin could have taken too many sleeping pills, lost consciousness in the shower, fallen and fractured his skull. Danger had a pulse. No, she did not relish the idea of being under the same roof as Paul and Annette, not even for a day, but she would endure it. She would listen to her mother's endless stories. She would eat and drink with them. She would agree with whatever ridiculous comments they made. She would play every role except that of a prodigal daughter. She did not need them; they were the ones who wanted her to visit. After seven days, she would say goodbye to her parents and Haiti. Perhaps she would return in a decade or two, or perhaps never.

When she reached the immigration counter and gave the agent her American passport, her heart started to race. Soon she would be released into Haiti's bruised arms. She wondered what would happen to her and Amber once they left the safety of the airport. Annette had said she would come fetch her, but what if something prevented her from coming? What if there had been an accident? What if her mother had been kidnapped on her way to the airport? What if there was a coup? What if there was another earthquake?

As she walked toward the baggage claim, Jacqueline's imagination busied itself with images of the chaos Kevin had described. If no one came to fetch her at the airport, she would be on her own. She would have to find ways to keep Amber safe. What would she do? She would not recognize the streets; she would be as blind as the moon.

As a child, she had been driven to school and home. She was ten years old when she left Haiti—she knew nothing of the country. She could see Kevin shaking his head at her stupidity. She wished she had taken his advice and convinced her parents to meet her in Miami instead. Something in her wanted to run back into the airplane and hide. She could see Kevin laughing at her now, telling her how silly she was to think she would have been safe in Haiti. She held Amber closer. She would be strong. Nothing would happen to her or her daughter.

"Could this be my little angel, Amber? *Ma petite fille*, you are a big girl," Annette cooed as she glided toward them. Paul followed with caution.

"Hello, Annette," Jacqueline said.

"Is that how you greet your mother after all this time?" Annette scooped up Amber in one swift motion. "My lovely angel."

Jacqueline kissed her mother on both cheeks.

Annette's pearl necklace captured Amber's interest. The child took the beads between her fingers.

"Leave your grandmother's jewelry alone." Jacqueline's voice was stern. It surprised her that Amber behaved as if she had seen Annette every day of her life—blood recognized blood.

"*Laisse ma petite fille tranquille,*" Annette scoffed, then flashed a perfect smile. Jacqueline hoped her mother would keep smiling, even if an excited tug on her pearls would scatter them like corn kernels in a chicken coop.

"*Comme tu es jolie!*" Paul remarked. He opened his arms to take Amber from his wife. The child screamed and shook her head. With tears suddenly streaming down her cheeks, Amber reached for Jacqueline and locked her arms around her mother's neck. Unsteady on his legs, Paul nearly toppled over.

Annette swerved sharply, waving manicured fingers dismissively. "Next time, maybe you will listen to me." And to Jacqueline: "He never listens to me. Let him fall and break his teeth. I told him to stay at the house, but he refused to listen. Pachou is very busy today. He could not play chauffeur." She smiled at Amber. "He's not too steady on those legs, you know. That wheelchair does nothing but collect dust at the house. Why he won't sit in it, I don't know." She took her husband by the arm, as if he could not walk by himself.

The four of them turned toward the exit. Annette gasped when she realized Jacqueline had only the small suitcase. "Is that all you brought?"

"Yes."

"What are you going to wear?"

"We're here only for seven days."

"But you still need to dress properly, yes?"

It had been so long since Jacqueline was in her mother's presence that she had forgotten how unalike they were. Jacqueline's idea of dressing properly meant the black jersey dress she had purchased at a sidewalk sale several years before Amber was even conceived. The sleeves came down to her wrists, and the hem stopped just above her ankles. The neckline left just the right amount of space for her string of lapis lazuli beads. Had there been nine more dresses in her size on the rack that day, she would have purchased them as well, and considered her wardrobe properly updated for at least another decade.

Paul's face contorted with discomfort as they headed toward the car. Annette leaned close to Jacqueline's ear and pretended to whisper, but spoke loudly enough for her husband to hear: "He's even more stubborn now than he was before the earthquake."

"I don't like it when you talk about me like I'm some deaf kid," Paul muttered.

"You might not be deaf, but you do act like a hard-headed child," Annette shot back. And to Jacqueline she added: "The Rock of Gibraltar is a cotton ball compared to that man's head." Annette laughed the rest of the way to the car. When they reached it, Paul held on to the side of the roof to pull his weight into the passenger seat. Annette took the wheel and began negotiating her way home.

Against her mother's wishes, Jacqueline rolled down the window. She wanted to see what she'd missed in twenty-five years. Trucks carrying orange-colored dirt drove recklessly, blaring their horns at pedestrians who shouted insults in return. The pungent smell of sweat mixed with live chickens tied feet-to-feet was overpowering. Half-dressed children weaved in and out of the wild traffic with five-gallon buckets on their heads.

"There's President Aristide's old residence," Annette announced, indicating a house on the left side of the road. "He's still in there, I think. He can't move an inch without someone watching. He's not permitted to receive visitors. He's on lockdown. Solitary confinement. No one goes into that house. No one comes out."

Paul asked, "What would you know about that?"

Annette ignored the question. She pointed to a reddish building with large windows and said, "That's the new American Embassy. Tell me it's not beautiful! Just the kind of building Haiti needs. It's very modern, artistic."

"It's an eyesore!" Paul yelled. "It's a fort. We don't need countries building forts in every corner. The United States, Chile, France, Philippines, and a whole bunch more built a least one fort in Haiti. And that's just for starters. They all came to help the Caribbean's *enfant terrible* out of its perpetual struggle. They liked the poverty so much they stayed."

"We need all the forts we can get." Annette swept her hands across the windshield to indicate the crowd popping about like corn in hot grease. "We had to build a wall to keep them from jumping into our swimming pool. They act like we built our house for them to use."

"That wall was a waste of money," Paul said.

"Thieves stole the concrete blocks before the cement could dry," Annette elaborated. "Stall keepers now use pieces of our wall as display counters for their wares. Tell me again why we don't need forts? You should see the holes they made in our brand-new security wall. Anyone can walk right through."

The car nearly tipped on its side when Annette swerved to avoid hitting a girl with a large basket centered on her turban. The skinny girl leaped sideways, losing her balance as well as her merchandise. The turban stayed glued to her cornrows. Rivulets of sweat coursed along her face. Several pedestrians swarmed the girl's basket and snatched as many pouches of water as they could before disappearing into the throng. "Roll up that window quickly," Annette commanded. Jacqueline did as told.

Out of nowhere a group of children appeared, many of them carrying large baskets of water pouches on their own heads. They rushed toward the girl, who was now trying to recover what remained of her inventory. The children helped her lift the basket back to the top of her head. She thanked them, and then shouted through gritted teeth a litany of insults in Annette's direction. Paul lowered his window to apologize, although his wife's eyes glinted like a knife's sharp edge.

"Unbaptized slut!" the child's angry voice rang inside the car. "Your crotch is full of maggots!" She cocked one hand on her bony hip and held her basket in place with the other.

"Stay-with pig!" Annette stuck her head halfway out of the driver's-side window, screaming, "*Rèstavèk!*"

"*Vini,*" Paul summoned the girl to the passenger side. "How much for one pouch of water?"

"*De dola,*" she said, craning her neck to see inside the car. When Amber smiled, the girl scowled.

"Sell me one," Paul said. The girl looked at him suspiciously before reaching into the basket on her head and producing a pouch of water. He paid with US currency.

The girl examined the bright green twenty-dollar bill, making sure it was not counterfeit. "*Ki betiz sa a? W ap pase m nan kaka?*" She shook her head violently and screeched, "What is this insult? What is this joke? Are you trying to smear shit on me? How am I supposed to find change for this amount of money?"

Paul winked. "If you can't make change now, save it for me. I'll come back to collect it tomorrow."

"How would you know where to find me?" the girl asked.

"If I don't find you, then I don't find you," Paul said, and shooed her away with a wave of his hand. The girl smiled and disappeared into the crowd.

Annette pushed on the horn as she drove, leaving a cloud of dust in her wake. "Why did you give that stay-with *macaque* our good money?"

"She would have been beaten for losing the merchandise," Paul said. "You know that as well as I do."

Annette adjusted the rearview mirror to assess Jacqueline's reaction. "If I end up in the streets of Port-au-Prince with a basket on my own head, Jacqueline, your father will be the reason. The man wants to toss everything we own into a bottomless collection plate. He would use our last drop of drinking water to extinguish Haiti's fires. And I'm supposed to let him do it without a word of protest."

"You're the one who almost ran over the girl," Paul bit back. "I saw that girl from a mile away. I never would have gotten so close to killing her."

"Save those words for the day when you get back in the driver's seat," Annette hissed. Looking in the rearview mirror again, she addressed Jacqueline: "Do you see how easily your father sides with complete strangers? He's become a mystery to me. Since that quake struck this country, Paul betrays me every chance he gets."

As they drove through Petion-Ville toward the Florestant house high in the hills, Jacqueline was surprised to discover that the serene road of her childhood had become a noisy bazaar, with mountains of discarded soda cans and bottles, used diapers, Styrofoam plates, and thousands of empty rice bags festooned with their *Made in the USA* logo. She wondered if that change had taken place before or after the earthquake. Perhaps the street vendors had lost their homes and families, and had no other place to sell their merchandise.

"Things are not what they used to be," Annette lamented. She gave a long, theatrical sigh; disdain reverberating in her voice. "It's horrible here. Some of our neighbors had to hire extra security to patrol their properties. Trespassers do what they please nowadays. They jump into our swimming pools and dare homeowners to complain. Property rights are a joke now in this country, unless you carry a gun. They break into houses, take food from refrigerators, steal jewelry, walk out wearing clothes from our closets, and call that democracy."

"No one has broken into our house," Paul countered. "Your mother has a wild imagination. No one would dare trespass on our property, and Annette knows it."

Kevin's many warnings sprang to Jacqueline's mind. She wondered if perhaps she should have listened to him and not come, but then she took comfort remembering that Leyla would join her the next day. Leyla knew Haiti as well as Paul and Annette. Jacqueline reasoned that her friend would be the ultimate guide and protector.

"Not yet!" Annette volleyed back. "Yes, tell us, Monsieur Paul Florestant, my dear! Who would stop these democracy-seekers if they did jump into our swimming pool or moved into our bedroom? Would you be the hero again? Would they listen to you like those employees you tried to save when that building crushed your legs?"

Paul let the insult slide like water into a drain. "If you're trying to scare Jacqueline and Amber, you're doing a good job. Why do you want to make it seem like everyone in Haiti is a criminal?"

"It's just like you to side with criminals, Paul. Why am I not surprised?" She turned her attention back to the open market bordering each side of the busy street. "Instead of birds singing in the morning, now I hear stall keepers squawking at customers to come buy their garbage. This country has changed. My *belle époque* is gone. Before the marketplace started to spread like a malignant tumor, our street was like a postcard. Now look at the heaps of junk!" Annette shook her head in disgust, then swerved again to avoid hitting a market woman.

"*Lonbrit pouri!*" the woman yelled. "*Dyablès. Lougawou.* I'll get you one day, I'll get you and your whole stinking family!"

"I'll get someone to gouge out your eyes," Annette spewed violently. Paul reached under his wife's arm to push on the horn in the middle of the steering wheel, scattering vendors and their customers. Women with heavy baskets balanced on their heads ran as if they were being chased by wild dogs.

"That's two people you nearly killed today," Paul said.

Annette *tsked*.

Amber giggled and clapped her hands excitedly. Jacqueline was thankful the child did not sit tall enough to see the blood-spattered pails of goat heads with teeth grinning like the butcher had tickled them silly before the cleaver came down.

"Nighttime is worse." Annette would not be stopped. "They've opened so many nightclubs and restaurants to entertain and feed the peacekeepers and help-givers, we're running out of space to stick a small-headed pin. Loud music plays until dawn. Our quiet neighborhood has turned into a vulgar dance hall. Male and female hookers are getting younger and younger. They strut around the marketplace and barter with their flesh, using private parts like penny slots."

"You still couldn't pay me to live anywhere else," Paul responded.

"That patriotism cost you one half of your body. One of these days it'll take the other half. If you'd listened to me long ago, we would have been enjoying a nice meal with civilized people when that damn earthquake struck. You wouldn't have had the accident. You'd still be . . . you."

Jacqueline listened without interrupting her parents.

"Drop the National Anthem act," Annette continued. "No one's going to invite you to sing and dance at the palace. That building is gone, like your good sense."

"Start a timer, Jacqueline," Paul said. "Let's count how long your mother can go without insulting me."

Annette was too consumed with her own thoughts to hear him. "Tell me that marketplace is not a jungle with all kinds of sick animals running around."

"I'm not telling you anything," Paul struck back. "Sooner or later your motor mouth will run out of gas. It'll get stuck somewhere, and I wouldn't count on me to help you." He did not laugh.

Annette shot him an angry look, then went on speaking animatedly: "Just last week they found a dead boy under a pile of rotten papaya and grapefruit. Naked as a newborn he was. Someone must have discarded him like a broken toy."

Paul pressed his index finger against his lips. "Annette, that's enough, yes?" He turned to look at Jacqueline and Amber. The child was engrossed in the commotion going on outside of the back window.

Jacqueline said, "That's fine, really. Baltimore City is not exactly paradise either." She thought about the missing and exploited children in America whose dated photographs stared from the back of milk cartons and grocery store circulars. *Have You Seen Me?* the captions always read. The dead boy in the marketplace would never make it to the back of a milk carton. She felt vulnerable suddenly—a circus performer attempting her first unicycle ride on a tightrope without a safety net. She tried not to imagine the swarm of flies that must have covered the fruit and the dead boy; but as an artist, every significant image was a potential story that needed to be told.

The eight-foot wall surrounding the property was topped with shiny razor wire—the double-edged kind one might find at a maximum-security prison. The wire was mostly concealed under lush branches of breadfruit trees. Every week without fail, at least one hungry passerby used to cut himself trying to pilfer breadfruit. Now, they just slipped through the holes in the wall and harvested a few.

Annette entered a numeric code on the panel next to the gate and waited for it to open. She drove slowly and watched the gate close behind the car through the rearview mirror. The drive from the front gate to the house was a winding road flanked by rosebushes and orchids—a banquet of nectar for the preponderance of butterflies that ushered them to their front door. Halfway to the house was a pond in which water lilies bloomed. It was paradise.

Jacqueline exhaled, and felt the muscles in her face relax into a smile. She squeezed Amber's arms and cooed softly, "We're here. This is Mommy's old house."

As they walked toward the front door, a memory returned: Annette telling her to bring Amber's umbilical stump to be placed under a breadfruit tree for safekeeping. Jacqueline had refused, saying it was an archaic ritual. But just in case there was an ounce of validity to the practice, she had put Amber's umbilical stump in the safest place she knew—though she would never disclose the location to Annette. Kevin did not know about this—he would have laughed at her and called her a superstitious Haitian.

All types of mangoes dangled from branches. There were cherry and grapefruit trees. One could live on the Florestant property for months without going hungry.

On the wraparound porch, lush ferns cascaded from hanging baskets. Flame vines with brilliant orange pendants covered the awnings. Jacqueline felt a weight on her chest. Her eyes moistened. Amber bounced in her arms, pointing her finger at everything she saw, screeching non sequiturs, smiling a wider smile than Jacqueline had ever seen.

With the exception of the ramp that was installed after her father's accident, the house and verdant grounds were as Jacqueline remembered. This was the house she often dreamed about. The landscape was the subject of most of her paintings. She felt a lump in her throat, and blinked back tears. Now she really wished Kevin was by her side. He should have been with her and Amber. She wanted him to see with his own eyes that her personal Haiti was not the wasteland he believed it to be.

Stepping onto the front porch, Jacqueline was six years old again. She was rushing home from school, ballet, or was it a piano lesson? There she was in a pretty pink-and-green floral-print dress, with satin ribbons in her hair, tearing into the neatly wrapped boxes under a decorated Christmas tree. Now she was in the salon, impressing Annette's affluent friends with her impeccable manners. She recalled the last time she stood on that porch, waving goodbye to the maids and to Pachou, the groundskeeper. He had done his best not to cry.

Jacqueline was seven years old now, stretching her fingers across the piano keys to play legato and staccato simultaneously. *Hear that!* Annette, nose up in the air, said to her guests. *Jacqueline Florestant is an ingénue!* A parent sneered at her own child, admonishing her, *You've been taking piano lessons for as long as Jacqueline has, you have the same teacher—why aren't you half as good?*

Annette never told her friends how many hours Jacqueline was made to practice each day. The girl's fingers would turn blue and her eyes would be raw with scalding tears. Of course Jacqueline learned to play brilliantly—she had to. One touch of the wrong key meant additional time on the piano bench; additional time in Chopin's prison. Jacqueline played like the protégée she was—not for the love of music, but to avoid punishment. Both Annette and Paul had been accomplished pianists. They could detect a false note from a thousand miles away.

After piano practice, there were language lessons, Latin and French. Latin was a bit challenging, but French was easy. Everyone, including the maids, spoke French. Any member of the household help who violated the French-only rule met with Annette's wrath. She fired a few maids for that one infraction. The Florestant house was her personal Palais National. Anyone who did not obey Annette's rules needed to disappear. Anyone except Pachou, the groundskeeper. He did not speak French, but she could never rid herself of him.

Pachou never learned to speak French, and would not

pretend otherwise. He had never gone to school, and did not plan to sit in anybody's classroom at sixty-two years of age. He lived in a two-room cinder-block house at the far end of the Florestant property. He was as much a fixture there as Annette and Paul. Pachou was born there, and was just a few years younger than Annette. His mother had worked as a maid in the house. She had died when Pachou was eight years old, and he continued to live on the property; now his roots reached as deep into the earth as the breadfruit trees. Pachou grew up alongside Annette. They could have passed for siblings, but never once played together as children are wont to do. That had been strictly forbidden. He was the help; she was the child of the house.

Amber smiled as her eyes took in the captivating panorama. There was a rustle from behind a hedge of roses, and out came Pachou with a machete in his right hand. He approached cautiously, squinting in the bright sun. "Is that little Jacqueline I see before me?"

She had smelled Pachou even before she saw him. Sweat poured from his head. A threadbare shirt was plastered to his chest. There were woodchips in his wooly hair. Calloused toes protruded from gaping holes in his battered and muddy shoes. He had many scars on his arms and a few fresh cuts. The caked blood mixed with dirt made him look like he had scales.

"And who is the little one in your arms?" he asked.

Amber screamed and hid her face behind the palms of her hands. Instinctively, Jacqueline drew her daughter closer to her chest. The look in Annette's eyes told Pachou he needed to be elsewhere; his presence was not welcome now.

Pachou disguised his humiliation with a grin, and stammered: "Annette, tell the little one there that I've never even killed an ant." He offered a grisly smile.

Amber kept her face hidden behind her hands. She had never seen anyone like him in her life. The groundskeeper glared at Annette while he apologized to Jacqueline for his sweat-covered clothes, his shoes with the holes in them, and the unpleasant smell that emanated from his skin. Annette fired another warning shot with her eyes. Pachou ignored that one too, and grinned.

"If you came here yesterday, I would have been my usual beautiful self," Pachou said, not looking at Annette. "But today is June 24, Saint John's Day. I have to deal with those trees before nightfall."

Jacqueline stared blankly. She did not understand what he meant, but decided against asking.

Pachou tipped an imaginary hat in Jacqueline's direction. "You must be exhausted, little Jacqueline. Rest and I'll see you later. I have to get back to the trees."

"Stop calling her *little Jacqueline*," Annette barked in French. "Does she look like a child to you? You may call her *Madame*. She is an adult, married, and has a child."

Pachou scratched the side of his head, exclaiming loudly, "I must be an old man now because little Jacqueline is a married lady! And a mother!"

Jacqueline managed a half-smile, and in Creole she said: "That's me, a married lady."

Annette flashed Pachou another murderous look.

"Is the husband here?" Pachou asked, looking around.

"There was an emergency situation at his job. He wanted to come, but unfortunately he could not," Jacqueline lied.

"Your husband is Haitian, yes?"

"American," Jacqueline replied.

"Is that okay with you, Pachou?" Paul asked in a good-humored tone.

Pachou shook his head, laughing a small laugh. Another cold look from Annette, and the groundskeeper swallowed hard, turned on his heels, and started in the direction of the trees. It would be dark soon, and there were still many fruit trees on the property to strike twenty-four times with the dull edge of his machete. If he touched a tree after dark, it would become barren. Everyone knew that.

FOURTEEN

S tanding on the porch, Jacqueline surveyed the lush vista. There seemed to be a breadfruit tree for every molecule of air. There were also almond, tamarind, cherry, kenèp, and guava trees. A maid stood nearby, smiling meekly, waiting for Annette's next command.

"Let's go inside," Annette said.

"What's the rush?" Jacqueline asked. She was suddenly reluctant to venture into the halls of a painful childhood.

"Aren't you the least bit interested in seeing your house after so many years?"

"I will in a minute," Jacqueline replied. She lowered herself into one of the throne-like white wicker chairs on the porch. Amber sat on her lap, resting her head on Jacqueline's chest as if it were a pillow.

In that moment, Annette peeled Amber from Jacqueline's chest in a motion so swift that there was no time to protest. She held Amber before her like the prow of a ship. "She looks like me," Annette gushed, daring anyone to disagree.

"She looks exactly like you," one of the maids said. The other bobbed her head in agreement.

Annette eyed both of them with disdain. "Why are you standing here like idiots? Isn't there something you should be doing inside the house?"

The maids bowed their heads and rushed toward the double doors that led into the salon. They did not go far—they waited close enough to the door to hear what was being said on the porch.

"The women were only admiring Amber," Paul said. "They're almost as happy to see her as we are. Who can blame them? Has anyone ever seen a more beautiful child?"

"That's the third time today you've sided with outsiders instead of being loyal to your wife. What do you want our daughter to think? Next thing you'll invite Pachou to eat with us in the dining room. Would you have me play the piano for him too? Go on and ask him what he wants for dinner."

Amber stirred in Annette's arms. Her eyes surveyed the environment with confusion and delight.

"*Bonjour, ma petite fille. Comment ça va? T'as besoin du lait? Des jouets? Des ballons?*" Annette cooed at her.

Amber stared at her grandmother blankly. Jacqueline expected her daughter to reach for her, but that did not happen.

"*Qu'est ce que tu veux?*" Annette continued pattering. "*Dis moi, ma petite princesse.*"

"She doesn't speak French," Jacqueline said.

"Mommy!" Amber shrieked, pointing her finger excitedly. "Mommy, Mommy, look! Blue turkeys. Blue turkeys, Mommy." A couple of peacocks dragged their extravagant trains behind them coquettishly. When they raised their feathers into colorful arcs, Amber applauded.

Annette cried out with delight as well and carried Amber toward the birds for a closer inspection.

"I want the blue turkey," Amber chanted, wriggling to

free herself from Annette's arms. Her eyes sparkled and her face became animated with a bright smile.

"*Ils sont charmants, n'est-ce pas vraie?*" Annette asked, pride lifting the corners of her mouth.

"She doesn't understand a word you say," Jacqueline reiterated. "We speak English at home. I plan to start teaching her Creole soon."

"You need to teach Amber to speak French, Jacqueline. The girl needs to be able to communicate with her *grandmère*. She needs to be cultured."

"Teach her German," Paul cut in. "Teach her Arabic or Japanese. She'll get more use out of those, God knows that's true."

"Both of you speak English fluently," Jacqueline said. "Speak to her in English. She's American through and through."

"That's hardly her fault," Annette scoffed, then sighed like an opera diva in a death scene. "You're not Haitian unless your umbilical stump is buried under a tree in this country—*this* country. Who knows what you did with my grandchild's *lonbrit?*"

Jacqueline glanced around, feigning incredulity. "Where did Annette Florestant go? She was here just a moment ago. Who is this superstitious fuddy-duddy that took her place?"

Paul laughed. "That woman comes and goes. You never know when she'll just vanish and this creature will take her place."

Annette curled her lips inward and crinkled her face, transforming herself into an old, toothless woman. She wiggled her index finger and in a grave voice admonished, "*S im te konnen toujou dèyè.*" She tiptoed a few paces, repeating the old aphorism: "Wisdom always comes too late."

Jacqueline rolled her eyes. Annette did not need to remind her that even though Amber was born on US soil, Haiti was still in her blood. "Haitians, especially girls, must be as strong as the breadfruit's roots. We bear fruit—and I'm not talking about babies." She tapped her barely-there belly with one hand and her left temple with the other. Paul looked bored. Annette continued: "Now, your father is a good example. Some might think he was a hero, but take a closer look. Who drove the car through Port-au-Prince's filthy streets today?"

"Yes, Jacqueline, listen to your *mamman*," Paul chimed in with a smirk. "Without women like this one here, Haiti would have fallen apart over two hundred years ago."

"Precisely!" Annette bellowed. "I've told you a thousand times, Jacqueline, your own *lonbrit* is here. That is why you're indestructible. Like our little *patrie*, yes?"

Jacqueline gave a faint smile. She agreed with Annette's assessment that the little *patrie* had shown signs of indestructibility. Haiti was not in the best of health, but she had a strong pulse.

As much as Annette had wanted Paul to stay away from Haiti for a while longer after his accident, she could be a staunch nationalist when the occasion called for it. Annette Florestant was a daughter of the island. Her *lonbrit* was buried under a breadfruit tree on the property too. But those who didn't know her might not have guessed it. Her almond-shaped eyes had traces of all the distant wonders of the world. Jacqueline contemplated her decision to do as she had chosen with Amber's *lonbrit*. Annette would probably faint if she knew her granddaughter's umbilical stump was at the bottom of the Potomac River, in a little box made of jade and gold. *No place on earth is safer than the river that runs by the capital of the most powerful nation in the world*, Jacqueline thought.

"Blue turkeys!" Amber exclaimed, clapping her hands.

"Peacocks are stunning creatures," Paul remarked in French-accented English. Amber continued to point at the birds. When suddenly she let out a piercing cry, all eyes swiveled in the direction of her pointing finger.

"Bastard," Annette mumbled loud enough for everyone to hear.

Pachou, machete over his right shoulder, was back from dealing with the trees. Amber darted toward Jacqueline, while Annette bolted toward Pachou. The maids, Paul, Jacqueline, and Amber were too far away to hear the conversation, but guessed it was not pleasant.

Staring into Patchou's rusted eyes, Annette's voice was an angry whisper, though her Creole was flawless. "My grandchild doesn't like you. You terrify her. Make yourself invisible for a few days. We won't need to see you. Do you understand?"

Pachou lowered the machete from his shoulder and considered its length and the condition of the blade. After one day of threatening trees, the blade was dull, but sharp enough to stop an enemy. Annette took a step back. Being near her made him feel as if there were worms in his pores. Still, the eyes that looked at her betrayed nothing. Annette grimaced, letting Pachou know that standing so close to him made her just as ill. He reached with his sawdust-covered hands to touch her pearl necklace. She recoiled.

Pachou grinned. "Don't worry about me coming

around and scaring your precious children. Come tomorrow, you'll have much bigger problems, believe me."

"Is that so?"

"That is so," Pachou said. "I am going to meet with an important person in Petion-Ville tomorrow morning. That person knows my situation and will help get things right finally."

Annette looked hard at his face. "Go to hell."

When Annette returned to Amber and Jacqueline, she said, "The scary old owl will not bother my granddaughter ever again." But by then, Amber had already returned her attention to the peacocks. "She is curious to a fault," Annette said.

Jacqueline shrugged.

In a voice tinged with contempt, Annette added: "Curiosity is good to a certain point. Americans take it too far, in my opinion. They want to get into everybody's house and find out what you had for breakfast and dinner the night before."

"You sound paranoid," Jacqueline responded. "In America, children who are curious tend to be quite intelligent."

Annette laughed. "Thank God my mother is not here to hear you talk like this. That is ridiculous—overt curiosity is vulgar. We didn't teach you to be vulgar, so poor Amber must have caught it from your husband's side of the family. That's a shame, she's such a lovely girl."

Jacqueline kept her mouth closed, but she knew what her mother was thinking: she was foolish not to have married a Haitian man from the right family. And from their circle of friends, Jacqueline could have had her pick among dozens of suitable young men. She should not have married a foreigner, an outsider.

"I'll do my best to try and cure her," Annette said, and meant it.

Jacqueline smiled inwardly, knowing that by this time tomorrow Leyla would be there to rescue her. Annette would have to be the ultimate hostess, on her best behavior at all times. She would stay busy being elegant, charming, and ordering the maids around, leaving Jacqueline to enjoy herself.

FIFTEEN

In spite of the servants' protest, Jacqueline bathed Amber herself, dressed her in her favorite pajamas, read her *The Little Mermaid*, and sang "Under the Sea" until she fell asleep. Afterward, Jacqueline joined her parents in the salon, where the oversized chandelier's reflection shone like precious stones on the grand piano's immaculate black lacquer. The mammoth instrument looked new, just as it had years ago when Jacqueline was Amber's age.

Back then, Annette had made her play for hours to entertain her friends. Tonight, however, it was Paul who serenaded the two women with every note his fingers could recall of "Fantaisie Impromptu" in C sharp. There was a tender look in his eyes, but his back was hunched over the keys, as if he would collapse at any moment. The fingers that used to move effortlessly across the keys were now reluctant and tentative.

Jacqueline looked at the quilted leather piano bench and recalled the hours she'd been forced to sit there; her bottom hurt as if the seat were bare wood. Every day after school, she practiced for many hours. On Saturdays, when her friends were in the swimming pools, running and playing, she was pinned to the piano bench. Paul would not allow her to move from it until she played like the ingénue he needed her to be.

Jacqueline was gifted, but the piano never truly interested her. She played because that was expected of her. Children from families like hers played the piano, danced ballet, and sang *chansonêttes*. Whether or not they possessed any talent was inconsequential. Jacqueline had not touched a piano in years, and chuckled at the mental image of how Annette would react if she learned that her star player had mastered the art of avoiding the piano.

Paul continued his lackluster performance, but soon grew tired. He had not so much as glanced at the piano since the earthquake had rattled his soul and cost him his legs. He knew he was not the only one who had lost so much in the quake, but he couldn't help feeling unlucky. When he went into town now, he saw dozens of amputees begging on the streets. He had never noticed so many in the past. Now, he saw them everywhere. He wondered how they lived. Did they have jobs? In the States, the blind could live independent lives. They went to work, took buses and trains. They listened for the sound of traffic lights changing. They could not be so independent in Haiti. There were no depressions in the sidewalks to accommodate wheelchairs or a blind person's cane. Wheelchairs were useless on roads with legendary potholes. He knew a few people who had wheelchairs, but they did not rely on the country's benevolence toward the disabled. Those friends lived in houses with smooth marble floors and elevators that took them to opulent rooms upstairs.

Haiti had changed since the earthquake, Paul lamented. In fact, the country had not been the same since most of his old friends in the government were forced to leave in the late eighties. He remembered the Haiti where one could put a gold watch on the hood of a car overnight and find it in same spot in the morning. He longed for that Haiti, and hoped that someday the old way would be restored. The presidents who had been his friends were now dead or in exile. Today's procession of supposed leaders did not possess the sophistication of previous governments. The new crop of presidents and interim presidents were crude, unrefined nouveau riche farmhands who had never heard about decorum and geniality. Paul was ashamed of them all, but would never leave his birth country.

His fingers now ached so much that he had to stop playing. They sat facing one another in a silence so awkward it was physically painful.

Jacqueline's mind was fixed on Kevin. She imagined him sitting with them in the salon—he would have been miserable. Paul's labored piano playing would have forced Kevin to shatter the quietude with questions.

Jacqueline would never forget the last time Kevin and her family were in the same room. It was at Amber's baptism, four years before. After the ceremony and reception, Kevin had turned to Annette and asked, "Just out of curiosity, what did it feel like to send your only child to boarding school thousands of miles away from home?"

Annette's eyes had flickered like faulty lightbulbs. She cleared her throat and said, "I beg your pardon?"

Jacqueline had turned in Kevin's direction and peered sharply into his eyes to let him know the road he was treading on was peppered with explosives.

Kevin stayed silent and Annette waved her delicate fingers dismissively, then said, "You are an ill-bread American. You are uncouth and savage. I should ignore you, but because you are married to my daughter, I choose not to. Know this, however: the next time you open your mouth to insult me, remember that I am not the sort of person you want to disrespect. Where I come from, idiots like you have been known to disappear like slugs under a pound of salt."

"Since we're introducing ourselves," Kevin fired back, "I am your only grandchild's father. But that means nothing to you. Clearly you don't do the family thing. You had one child and dumped her like she was an inconvenience."

Annette's lips had trembled. Her eyes narrowed, but she said nothing more.

"Next time you think about insulting me," Kevin continued, "remember that I am one of the uncouth, savage Marines who kept your kind from being dumped into the same holes you dug for your enemies. And, by the way, your family name means absolutely nothing to me."

Yes, Jacqueline thought now, *it's just as well that Kevin stayed away.* He might say too much. He might ask too many questions. She smiled when she remembered once again that Leyla would be with her by this time the next day. She had already fulfilled the obligation to visit her father. Now she wanted to restock her memory, as Kevin put it, with the colors she needed to revive her canvases back home.

Her body was in the salon with her parents, but her mind left to be with Kevin. As much as he infuriated her sometimes, he was the man she loved—the father of the child for whom she would give her life without a second's hesitation.

After some time, Annette placed her drink on a silver tray near her chair and reached for a stack of photo albums.

On cue, Jacqueline rose to exit the salon. "Don't go," Annette bleated. "There's something I need you to see."

Jacqueline loved Annette as much as a daughter could love the mother who gave her away so she could see the world before it stopped spinning, but the idea of sifting through a bunch of photographs from bygone decades was unpleasant at best.

Annette smoothed the plastic sheets protecting the snapshots. In Jacqueline's mind, each picture was a shovel of dirt in the excavation of a childhood she had buried long ago. Her mother showed her picture after picture, reciting the names of this and that person, adding one anecdote after another—stories that reminded Jacqueline of the loneliness she felt as her mother hopped from plane to plane to make small talk with all the beautiful strangers of the world.

After an obligatory thirty minutes of sifting through old books of painful memories, Jacqueline excused herself and wandered out to the yard. A hammock suspended between two breadfruit trees by the pool called out to her. The moonlight gave the trees a surreal quality.

In the distance, loud music from the nightclub shattered what might have been a perfect moment. Ominous shadows danced on the water in the swimming pool. Despite the distraction, each time Jacqueline blinked, her eyes stayed closed a little longer. The hammock welcomed her body, rocking her like a baby in a bassinet. The night opened its warm arms to embrace her, and Jacqueline yielded.

In spite of her difficult childhood, it felt good to be on the property again. Amber was happy and mesmerized. Jacquline was certain that Kevin was at home seething, but she reminded herself that he'd had the option to join them. Her parents were getting old, Kevin should have been more considerate. The next time she came back might be to bury them. Once again, her mind veered toward Leyla.

Jacqueline's eyelids lowered until darkness was all that remained. She drifted to that place where memories blurred and took on distorted shapes. Below the black sky and not too far above the blacker earth—in that mysterious realm of the trees' far-reaching branches—fowls flapped their wings, thrashing in time with the frenzied rhythm pounding through the night. Sleeping leaves awoke and swooshed their discontent. A trogon screeched from her slumber atop four speckled eggs in a cozy nest. The music grew louder, and the dealings of sex workers with their customers reached such a pitch that the trees holding the hammock seemed to protest. The trogon's eyes flicked open. Her head jerked from side to side, surveying her manor. The music grew even louder. Just then a hawk dove toward the nest. The frightened trogon whistled loud enough to awaken the dead in the cemetery miles away.

Jacqueline jerked awake, and instinctively reached with her hand to touch whatever it was that had landed so close to her body. She could not see in the dark, but felt something slippery and foul-smelling. She leaped out of the hammock. The wetness in her hand felt like a gel—instinctively she knew it had to be blood. Grudgingly, Jacqueline rushed back into the house, taking care to keep her dirtied hand away from the rest of her body.

Walking past her parents' bedroom, she heard one of Annette's old *chansonêttes française* playing. She recalled how on Saturday afternoons between piano practice and preparing for the night's party, her mother would subject the household to Mireille Mathieu, Nana Mouskouri, Charles Aznavour, Edith Piaf, and others. Tonight, a host of angelic voices accompanied Mireille as she sang about a statue keeping watch over travelers on a turbulent sea. Annette's soprano seeped through the space under her bedroom door: "*La statue regarde la mer qui vagabonde . . .*"

Jacqueline went through her old bedroom to the bathroom. She turned on the faucet and scrubbed her hands, watching with disgust as blood ran between her fingers. And even though whatever had happened to the bird was not her fault, she felt somehow responsible. For a brief moment she considered going back to the hammock to see what—if anything—she could do to help the creature. Then she threw the idea out of her mind like a soiled towel into the laundry bin.

Amber was sleeping in the exact spot where Jacqueline had placed her hours before. She reclined next to her daughter now, marveling at this child who was truly hers. She had carried her inside her own body for nine months. When she had gone in for sonograms and saw the baby curled up inside of her, tears had flowed out of her eyes. Amber was born with her fists clenched and a wail so piercing it was as if she had seen something horrific in her first few seconds in the outside world. And Jacqueline knew, in that very instant, that she would never love anybody as much, including herself. She would be sure to tell her child every day how much she loved her. She would do anything to insure her baby's happiness—anything at all.

There they were tonight, mother and child, resting

side by side. There was no Kevin, who, like a thief, had fed Amber the breast milk that came from Jacqueline's body. She was the one who made the milk, pumped it out with a heavy machine; but he was the hero around whose fingers Amber curled her own when she fed. Jacqueline's smile grew wider. Tonight she was the one who got to bathe Amber, dress her, and comb her hair. Amber needed her, just as she had needed her breast milk as a baby.

Stretched on the bed close to her daughter, Jacqueline picked up the receiver and dialed home. Kevin would be glad to know that no machete-wielding madman had chopped off his angel's hair. His wife and child were safe, just as she'd promised him they would be.

He answered on the first ring. "How's Amber?"

"Asleep," Jacqueline whispered. She could tell Kevin had not touched his little fix-all pills. She knew he probably would not sleep until their family was together again. He would force himself to stay awake—just as he had learned to do in the war. Seven days and six nights, he could manage that. If he could stay awake in the desert, protecting strangers, he would do the same for his own child.

"Kiss my girl for me." Kevin's voice was tense.

Jacqueline kissed Amber and said, "Check." After a lengthy silence, she whispered, "I miss you."

"You made your choice."

"I love you." The words came out of her mouth like an apology, and Kevin quickly ended the call.

Jacqueline considered calling Leyla next, but decided not to. It was too late to start one of their marathon conversations. Even as she thought she should wait and call in the morning, her fingers dialed the number mechanically.

"How's my best friend?" Leyla asked in a groggy voice. "How's the heat been?"

"So far so good. It's almost as beautiful as I remembered."

"I told you so. How are the folks?"

"They're getting old, you know. They're not the fierce and formidable people I knew as a kid."

"Time has a way of calming people down."

"I wish you were already here," Jacqueline allowed.

"I'll be there tomorrow. Go on and tuck yourself in. You're going to need all your energy tomorrow."

"Don't forget Pachou will pick you up from the airport. He'll have a sign with your name on it."

Leyla laughed. "How will I know the person holding the sign is the real Pachou."

"You'll have to just trust him," Jacqueline said, laughing also.

SIXTEEN

A soft rain fell during the night, christening anew every petal of the rosebushes below Jacqueline's bedroom window. A sweet fragrance permeated the room. Promptly at sunrise, an eager band of parakeets, palm chat, and mourning doves featured a certain soloist named Amber Marshall. The stage consisted of pillows stacked against the headboard. The diva reached out of the window with both hands to try and embrace her enchanting new world.

"Mommy, Mommy . . ." Amber sang loudly, holding the discordant notes for what seemed like hours.

Sleep was so sweet in Jacqueline's eyes that she was determined to keep it there. She tried to ignore her little superstar, but could not. "Quiet, Amber! Let Mommy rest."

Five more minutes of sleep was all Jacqueline wanted. It had been too long since she'd slept in her old room. Back in the States, there was concrete and steel outside her bedroom window. Here, she had a garden filled with glorious orchids and birds of paradise. The jasmine and gardenia were spellbinding.

Amber cared precious little for the garden's hypnotic perfume. Her only wish was to be outside where there was more sky and more earth than she had ever seen in her life. She loved the Florestant's lush tropical oasis. "Mommy, I want to stay here forever," she declared.

The peacocks! There was nothing with which to compare the striking flock. Amber had never seen blue so blue, gold so brilliant—not even in Jacqueline's paintings. "Mommy, Mommy," the child went on. She was unstoppable. "Where is Grandmère? I want to see blue turkeys!"

"*Rete trankil, pitit,*" Jacqueline groaned in Creole, her eyes still closed.

"I want Grandmère now." The only thing missing was a picket sign. The room shook with an I'm-going-to-die-unless-you-do-what-I-ask wail.

Jacqueline jumped out of bed, snatched Amber up in her arms, and sprinted down the hallway toward her parents' bedroom. She did not bother to knock. "She's all yours," she announced, and closed the door behind her.

Annette, in a powder-pink silk nightgown and matching robe that reached the floor, was at her vanity, applying cream under her eyes. Paul was on the porch, enjoying his morning coffee and reading the newspaper. Amber's eyes widened. The ornate and oversized furniture made the room look like it belonged in a fairy tale. The walls were an endless *trompe-l'œil* of the gardens of Versailles. The lights from twin crystal chandeliers reflecting in the many mirrors made the room sparkle. Amber twirled around in awe.

"Blue turkeys," she babbled to her grandmother, and pointed to the window.

Annette took the child's hands and pressed the palms against her own cheeks. How long had it been since such precious hands had touched her face? She regretted sending Jacqueline to boarding school so many years ago. She regretted having exchanged her only child for Machu Pichou, Istanbul, even Jerusalem. She had missed seeing Jacqueline grow into a woman, and for what? The marble Jesus was still in the Virgin Mary's marble lap somewhere inside Saint Peter's Basilica—neither had shifted position in five hundred years.

"We go outside, *oui?*" Amber said, tugging on her *grandmère's* arm. "Blue turkeys, *oui?*"

"Give me one moment," Annette replied in French. To distract Amber, she turned the radio on; the song about the statue guarding the sea played as it had the previous night. Annette spun like a ballerina inside a music box. Amber giggled and continued to twirl long after Annette had stopped dancing and disappeared behind her closet door. Rows and rows of dresses hung as if on racks in an upscale boutique. There were evening gowns from decades past, hat racks, and shelves full of shoes. Annette's closet was like one of the Florestant's department stores. Amber, dizzy from spinning, collapsed on the large bed with a cackle.

Annette chose sky-blue linen slacks and a white shirt. Then she studied her reflection in the mirror and did not approve of what she saw. She tried on khaki capris and a safari-style shirt. When she saw her waistline reflected in the mirrors, she made a mental note to keep away from the Grand Marnier for a few days. After two or three more changes, she decided the sky-blue linen slacks actually looked the best.

Annette was still in her closet when the last song on the CD reached a crescendo. Amber did the same, wailing: "Grandmère, Grandmère!" Annette was too deep inside the closet to hear, so Amber marched to the bedroom door, turned the knob, pulled it open, and sauntered out as if she had lived in the house since birth.

The birds called out to her. On one end of the porch, Paul sat quietly. Before him on the glass-topped white wicker table, there was an untouched glass of orange juice, toast on a white plate, a white napkin, and a silver sugar container with matching *cafetière* and creamer. He was too absorbed in an old news article to eat.

Amber tiptoed in the other direction, where the birds' song was loudest. She would join them, and could not wait. She held the balustrade as she made her way down the steps. Quietly, she jumped on the grass. Her eyes were bright with wonder. When she saw a peacock's magical plumage, she gasped, and ran toward it with outstretched arms.

The morning sun danced through the leaves of the breadfruit trees, making dappled patterns on the dew-drenched grass. The water in the swimming pool glittered like stars. The water must have known Amber's name, for it called out to her too. Amber could not wait to touch the peacocks. They would teach her how to fly; they would reveal to her how to grow magical colors.

Inside the house, Jacqueline was still intoxicated by the roses' perfume. She slept soundly, dreamlessly, drowning in sweet oblivion.

Amber made her way across the lush garden. The grass was slick with dew, causing her to lose her footing and slide a little. Giggling, she rose to her feet and continued her determined march toward the peacocks. They promised to reveal the secret of their magic; they would entertain her. She had never seen birds so elegant and delightful. Their vibrant colors mesmerized her. But something on the ground near the hammock piqued Amber's curiosity. She inched closer and saw that it was a little basket made of twigs and dried leaves. Upon closer inspection, she noticed the speckled eggs. She was delighted to discover what had to be the smallest birds in the world. Part of their bodies were inside the broken egg shells; the other parts—naked except for a few feathers—were outside. They seemed to be sleeping. They did not react to the flies buzzing around their small beaks and eyes.

From the mysterious world up in the breadfruit trees' branches a fierce wind blew, and a shadow flew. Amber looked up and tried to adjust her eyes, but the sun was overpowering. The hawk dove in her direction, beating its wings furiously. It hovered in the air, just above Amber, and in its eyes a violence shone that frightened her.

Amber ran backward. For a moment she forgot about the peacocks. The grass under her feet was like a waterslide. The hawk flapped its wings harshly. Amber screamed but no sound came through the terrible knot in her small throat. She ran faster, her arms flailing. She never looked at where she was going; she thought only of running and running and hoped the hawk would leave her be. But before that could happen, she slipped and fell with a gentle splash. The hawk turned away and returned to the breadfruit tree.

"Amber, Grandmère will take you to the garden now," Annette said from within her closet. She looked as if she was ready for lunch at the now shattered palace. "Where are you, darling?" she called out in French, looking around the opulent bedroom.

When Amber did not answer, Annette remembered how children found a game of hide-and-seek irresistible. "Come out, wherever you are." She looked behind the curtains, under the vanity table, under the bed, back inside the closet. "Amber, sweetheart, let's go see the magnificent birds now." She raised her voice a couple octaves, already losing patience and wishing Jacqueline had not brought the girl to her so early in the morning. When Amber still did not answer, Annette went to Jacqueline's room.

Jacqueline's arms were crossed on her chest, her fingers interlaced as if in prayer. There was a time long ago when she would have sensed her mother's presence, even as she slept. Not now. Annette could have stood inches from Jacqueline's face and she would not have known. Sweet oblivion.

Annette whispered, "Come out, darling. Let's go see the birds." She waited a few moments for Amber to respond.

When the child didn't, Annette went into the kitchen and asked a maid if she'd seen Amber.

"*Non*, Madame Florestant."

"*Merde!*" Annette snapped. Children could be adorable one minute and insufferable the next. She was enjoying having Amber at the house, but obviously the child had a few bad traits—no doubt inherited from her father. They hadn't been there twenty-four hours and already Annette, in spite of herself, was looking forward to the visit's end.

"Find Amber," she told the maids. "She's playing hide-and-seek." They searched the salon, the dining room, the breakfast room, and ended up back in the bedroom.

Jacqueline shifted her position on the bed—the hypnosis had broken. She went to the bathroom and looked at her face in the medicine cabinet's mirror. She was pleased with what she saw. She had slept peacefully, and would sleep that well again for all the nights spent at her parents' house. She yawned and her lips spread into a smile. She lifted the toothbrush from the counter, coated it with toothpaste, and turned on the faucet.

"Have you seen Amber?" Annette asked through the cracked door. "I've been looking for her everywhere. She must be hiding in the house somewhere. You know children love to play."

"I know," Jacqueline said. "But Amber knows not to play hide-and-seek. She did that at our place once; Kevin almost had a heart attack. She learned her lesson."

"Right, she's probably on the porch with Paul."

"Probably," Jacqueline agreed. "Well, let's go find our little angel."

"Have you seen Amber?" Annette asked Paul when they reached the porch.

"She's inside the house," he said, putting the newspaper on the table, his mind occupied with Haiti's rice problem and former President Bill Clinton's apology for his country's role in it. "I've not seen her, and I've been here for a while now."

Everyone went back inside the house, calling for Amber and getting increasingly concerned. For a brief second it occurred to Jacqueline that her child could have been kidnapped, but then she was instantly reassured by the fact that her parents' house was like a fort, in spite of the gaping holes in the security wall. Although the market people sometimes slipped through the open spaces to steal a breadfruit or relieve themselves, they would never dare come much closer. No one could enter the house without an invitation. Everyone knew people like the Florestants were armed and would not hesitate to defend themselves.

Pachou came out of his cabin dressed in a crisp shirt and slacks. He did not want to be late for his appointment; he had waited decades for this day. Finally, all that had been wrong in his life would be made right. And no one, not even Annette Florestant, could stop him from getting the respect he was due after a lifetime of penury and deprivation.

He walked stealthily past the pool, making sure no one at the house noticed him. He didn't need Annette's insults for breakfast. He could not wait to return to the house that afternoon with a new self—one whom Annette would have to acknowledge and respect—but something in the pool caught his attention. He leaned closer for a better look, and a scream ripped out of his throat.

The noise startled Annette. She watched with horror as the groundskeeper dove headfirst into her sparkling swimming pool. "Do you see that?" she shouted to Paul. "That filthy bastard is in our pool! Get the hell out of there, Pachou!"

Annette suspended her search for a moment and hurried toward the pool. When Pachou emerged with Amber in his arms, Annette had to blink several times to make sure she saw what her mind did not yet wish to register. Amber's arms fell to her sides. Pachou moved quickly, placing the child on the grass and trying to get the water out of her lungs.

"I'll get the doctor," he said, but they all knew a doctor would only confirm the obvious.

Amber's face was already gray. Her lips were drained of color. Her eyes stared at the sky and reminded Pachou instantly of Anaika Saint-Louis—the little girl he and dozens of other people had tried to save after the earthquake. He wondered how long she'd been in the pool before he found her. He looked at Annette. She stumbled as she ran toward them.

From the porch, Jacqueline saw Pachou kneeling on the grass next to Amber and flew toward them.

"What did you do to her?" Annette gasped. There was a storm in her eyes.

Pachou swallowed hard. He stammered, "She was in the p-pool. Deep in the bottom, and not moving. I took her out. I don't know how long she'd been there."

"Get away from her!" Jacqueline let out a guttural scream.

Paul craned his neck to see what was happening. His crutches were leaning on the railing. He took them, shoved one under each arm, and made his way toward the swimming pool. He was not wearing his prostheses.

"Call 911!" Jacqueline screamed.

Pachou looked around, confused. 911 did not exist in Haiti.

"Call the ambulance!" Jacqueline shrieked.

Shock can make a person forget the most basic facts. There was no public emergency number to call. There were doctors in a house nearby—but nearby meant a twenty-minute drive.

"Immediately!" Jacqueline was frantic.

The word *immediately* had a different definition in

Haiti. Things moved at the speed of the heat, slow and punishing. Even if someone needed to get somewhere in a hurry, the rubble that still covered the roads after the earthquake made traveling by car difficult and perilous.

When the doctor arrived it was forty minutes later, and he pronounced what everyone already knew.

Upon hearing the diagnosis, Jacqueline took off running in circles, screaming words no one understood. She pulled clumps of hair out of her head and tore the shirt from her skin. She scratched her face, digging with her nails into the flesh, making it bleed and sting, but she did not feel that pain.

Annette looked at her husband, searching for the right words. "The doctor said it happened very fast. She did not suffer."

"You don't know what you're saying!" Jacqueline chewed the skin around her nails, spitting out bits of flesh. Her face swelled as tears poured out of her eyes.

SEVENTEEN

L ater that day, Annette explained to her daughter that
she had meant to take Amber to the garden as soon as
Jacqueline brought her to the bedroom, but of course
she couldn't have risked being seen in her bedroom
clothes by strangers. It wasn't just the maids who might
have seen her. The stall keepers from the ever-expanding
marketplace and their customers had developed a habit
of crawling through the holes in the wall to relieve themselves behind the bushes and steal breadfruit.

Annette swore she had told Amber to wait for her as
she stepped into her dressing room to change out of her
nightclothes. "I was gone for less than a minute," Annette said, and believed her own lie. "Damn that bastard
Pachou. I hold him personally responsible for what happened. He's always been useless."

"I am the one who's useless," Paul whispered, tears
flowing freely. "I should have seen her come out of the
house. I should have been paying attention."

"Yes, you should have," Annette said bitterly.

Jacqueline was still pacing and mumbling incoherently.

Paul wanted to tell Jacqueline how much he loved her;
that his own heart was breaking. But he couldn't find the
words to speak. He lowered his eyes and tried to breathe
through the lump in his throat.

Disbelief spilled from Jacqueline eyes. Her knees buckled and she dropped on the ground as if someone had pushed and kicked her. Annette tried to lift her from the floor but she recoiled. Someone mentioned Kevin, and Jacqueline closed her eyes. She could not think about him now. Not yet. She might never call him. Telling him about Amber would make the nightmare real.

"Kevin needs to know," said Annette in a somber tone. "I'll make the call."

Jacqueline shook her head. It was up to her to make the call. But what would she say? What words would she use? This was one of those times when mouths don't speak.

Annette shot her husband another hateful look and reached for her daughter's hand, but Jacqueline pulled away. She screamed internally, through the shards of glass in her throat. She did not need a mother now. She did not want Annette Florestant near her. She felt the same toward Paul—they were both responsible for what had happened to Amber. She would be sure to tell that to Kevin. Kevin . . .

Yes, Kevin needed to know. Jacqueline wondered if his instincts had already delivered the news. Parents have a way of sensing these things. She thought back to the moment when Amber must have fallen in the pool. Did she feel something, anything at all? That detail eluded her now; that question would follow Jacqueline to her own grave and beyond.

Every eye was on her. Mothers who lose their children are unpredictable, unstable. She could fall asleep and will herself to awaken in the same unknown world as her child. She could break down doors and take to the streets running, tearing at her clothes and hair. Nothing anyone could say would undo agony's tight noose.

Kevin needed to know, but she could not tell him. Not now. Not yet. Miracles were still possible, Jesus said so. Amber could be revived like a modern-day Lazarus, and so many would believe again.

But first, Jacqueline needed to speak with Leyla. Leyla would know just what she should say to Kevin. Leyla might even tell Kevin for her. Jacqueline could not speak now—she was disintegrating.

With unsteady hands, she punched the speed dial on her cell phone. Every second was an eternity. She did not know where to begin. "Hello, Leyla," she said nervously.

"You sound like you've been hiking up to the Citadel. How was the climb?"

"It's Amber," Jacqueline began in a tremulous voice.

"Amber went up the Citadel?"

"She's gone." Jacqueline nodded, as if Leyla could see her. Somehow, saying the words made it even more real. She began to sob.

Leyla gasped. "Do you know who took her? Did they mention how much money they want? Whatever they ask, let's hurry up and pay before they get angry and desperate. Whatever you need, I'm here for you. I'll pawn everything I've got."

"No, no. Amber is . . . There was an accident. In the pool. She wanted to see the peacocks. She fell in the pool. She's gone."

"Jacqueline, don't say any more," Leyla sobbed. "I'll be there in a couple of hours."

Leyla took the next available flight, and arrived in Haiti

in less time than it would have taken to fly to Washington State. Pachou was dispatched to the airport, holding a cardboard sign with Leyla's name in bold letters. When she spotted him, she asked in Creole: "Who sent you?"

"Jacqueline Florestant."

"Tell me Jacqueline's parents' name," Leyla said curtly.

"Paul and Annette. Florestant."

"Where do they live?"

"Thunder strike me down, woman!" Pachou glared at her and sucked his teeth. "I don't have time for this game. Amber is . . . a child is . . . You want to come with me or not? I got no problem leaving you here."

"Let's go," Leyla said, and followed him to the car.

The silence was like dense fog inside the car. Pachou was curious about the lady in the backseat, but did not care to ask a question. The only thing on his mind was the morning's tragic event. Nothing else mattered, especially not some blue-eyed woman who asked too many questions. It was Leyla who shattered the silence, asking how long it would take before they reached the house.

"*Nan blokis sa a?*" Pachou replied with a question of his own. The roads were backed up for miles. It could take thirty minutes or three hours. "*Sa depan,*" he added. "If we have good luck, we'll reach the house in no time at all." He wished he had chosen his words better. This thing called *good luck* had been flung into a mass grave with thousands of nameless faces in the aftermath of the earthquake; that much he knew for certain.

They said nothing to each other for a few uncomfortable minutes. Finally Leyla gently punctured the silence: "The way the sun is shining makes it impossible to imagine that bad things could happen in this country."

Pachou had heard foreigners speak Creole before, but this lady, with her blond hair and blue eyes, sounded like she had lived in Haiti her entire life.

"It was a horrible accident," Pachou said. "If I'd been there in time, maybe I could have done something. I wish I had been there. I would have gotten her out of that pool." He shook his head.

Leyla watched him through the rearview mirror. The whites of his eyes were almost orange. His face was thin and angular. There were pleats around his mouth and on his forehead. His skin was black and shiny. She studied the hands on the steering wheel. They were calloused, and the knuckles were darker than the rest of his skin. He held the steering wheel with a tight, nervous grip— like someone holding a rope to keep from falling from a great height. She felt as if she had seen him somewhere before. She studied him as inconspicuously as she could. Something about him made her think of Jacqueline. His eyes were shaped like her friend's. She wondered if they were related, but told herself there was no way that was possible—the man was the groundskeeper.

"How is Jacqueline doing?"

"Not good," Pachou said. "She screams and holds her stomach. She paces, she screams, and she claws at her face. She pulls out clumps of hair. She cries."

Leyla knew. She had seen mothers lose their babies before; they almost always came unglued. She had lost her own unborn child, and she now wondered which pain tore a mother's inside worse: knowing the person you lost, or not knowing.

"It was a tragic accident." His voice was thin. "It was

nobody's fault. They say Amber came outside to see the peacocks."

"Peacocks?"

"Annette keeps them in the yard. Amber wanted to see them. She was probably running. She must have slipped and fallen."

Leyla suppressed a scream.

Pachou drove as if he were being chased by an angry mob. When they reached the house, he opened the passenger door and led Leyla to the front porch. A wave of gloom engulfed her as soon as they reached the doorway. Annette rose to meet them. She extended her hand, and Leyla wanted to embrace her, but restrained herself.

Jacqueline wanted to run to Leyla as soon as she heard her voice, but she couldn't move, so Annette delivered Leyla to her. Not a word passed between them. For now, they held each other quietly. Jacqueline convulsed while Leyla held her, making gentle circles on her friend's back. Pachou and the maids sat on the throne-like wicker chairs on the porch, rocking themselves back and forth without looking at one another or saying a word. Annette and Paul sat next to each other in the salon.

Paul stared out of the window, muttering to himself and swallowing sobs. The chair underneath him groaned. The house was filled from floor to ceiling with grief. The breadfruits' leaves, the roses, the peacocks, and even the furniture seemed to weep.

Annette held her chest and wept with elegance, but her eyes were dry as bones. "Why?" she asked no one in particular.

Jacqueline silently berated herself for taking her daughter to Annette's room that morning. If she had kept the child with her, she would be alive now. Jacqueline hated herself for having stayed up so late the night before, contemplating the shadows the breadfruit trees were throwing on the pool. She hated herself for swinging in the hammock without a care in the world. She might have slept right there under that deceitful moon if the half-eaten trogon had not fallen on her. She also despised her mother for disappearing into her closet for a costume change and leaving Amber unattended. If Annette had not been her usual vain self, Amber would not have gone outside alone, and she would still be alive. Annette was to blame for Amber's accident.

If the peacocks hadn't learned Amber's name, they would not have called out to her so early in the morning, and she would not have gone to them. The peacocks were to blame too.

Annette sat demurely, eyes on the fingers interlaced in her lap. She kept her mouth shut, but inside she seethed as she recalled telling Jacqueline—even while Amber was still in her womb—to bring the child's umbilical stump to Haiti. Her *lonbrit* should have been placed under a strong breadfruit tree for safekeeping, and the child would have been protected for one hundred years. Annette wanted to open her mouth and scream at Jacqueline for being so irresponsible and stubborn, but she restrained herself.

Jacqueline now fervently wished she had upheld the old tradition. Amber needed to be protected against life's many dangers. How could she have thrown her child's *lonbrit* in something as unstable and formless as water?

Blame was so thick and palpable that the air stood still. Annette bit her fingernails, chewing around the edges until bits of blood pooled there.

A hurricane of memories whirled inside Jacqueline's head. All Amber had wanted was to be with her *grandmère*. Wasn't that what she said?

"Kevin," Jacqueline whispered to Leyla. "Oh my God, Kevin . . ."

"You haven't told him?"

"No."

Leyla understood, and she sighed. She took Jacqueline's face in her hands and brought her head to rest on her chest. Leyla would call Kevin. She would deliver the news. He would hate her for it, she knew it. But that would spare Jacqueline the ultimate burden. Tears leaked out of Jacqueline's soul, and Leyla held her tighter.

Leyla dialed the number, as she'd done dozens of times since the day she and Jacqueline agreed to become teacher and student confidants. Kevin answered—as if he had been waiting for her call. His voice was flat, steeped in what sounded like resignation. Did he know?

"Kevin," Leyla began in a soft, apologetic voice, "this is Leyla . . ."

"What's going on?"

"There's been a terrible accident . . ."

"What the fuck is going on?" he demanded.

Leyla paused a second before starting again. "Kevin . . ."

"Put Jacqueline on!"

"She can't really speak right now."

"Then let me talk to Amber."

Leyla's eyes filled with tears and suddenly she found it impossible to speak. "Amber fell . . ."

"Talk, goddamnit!"

"There's been a terrible accident. In the pool. Amber fell in the pool."

"How is Amber? Is she in the hospital? Where is she now?"

"She's not in the hospital," Leyla said. "She's gone. It was an accident."

"Where's my daughter?" Kevin asked in a cold voice. Images from his months in the desert flooded his mind. He recalled a woman clad in black from head to feet, cradling another person executed by her own people in the name of love. Kevin's mind showed him footpaths strewn with bodies half-curled up in the fetal position. The people called out their mothers' names as they perished. Did they taste death? Had they kissed their lovers goodbye in time? Were the ones who were supposed to mourn them dead too?

Kevin's mind was a whir of unanswerable questions. He had been "discharged with honor" from the desert, but what did that mean? The desert followed him everywhere. The desert never set him free. Amber was the one who'd helped him forget the unbearable smell of rotting flesh, and the shrieks of the condemned. He despised the desert, but he was proud of having served his country when others had only googled the war. He despised himself for the role he had to play, but would not hesitate to pick up his weapon and return—if it meant Amber would not have to breathe poisoned air. He would inhale it all first, just to keep her alive.

Haiti was not Fallujah. There was no war. But he'd told Jacqueline the opposite: Haiti was always at war. The war, then, was to blame. Haiti was to blame. Jacqueline was to blame. Leyla was to blame. Annette and Paul were as guilty as they had always been. He hated them all for what they had done, or failed to do.

"Are you there?" Leyla asked.

Kevin did not respond. He flung the phone across the room. He did not know the details, but he knew he would never see his daughter alive again. He would never hear her laugh again. She would never ask him to read a bed-time story. She would never hold his hands and pull him toward whatever it was that she didn't trust her own eyes to believe. *Come see, Daddy. Come see.*

Kevin took a flight that afternoon and was in Haiti by evening. There was no time to be thankful for the fact that being a veteran afforded him a number of privileges. Airline personnel gladly moved his name to the top of the standby list.

As soon as he exited the airport, he threw himself into the backseat of a taxi. "Take me to—wait one moment. Crap!" He realized his in-laws' address was not on his contact list. He tried to remember some part of it, but couldn't. He dialed Jacqueline's cell, but the call went directly to voice mail. He dialed a second and third time, and got the same result. "Shit!" he exclaimed.

The driver looked straight ahead and said nothing.

"The police," Kevin said at last. "Maybe the police can help me find these people. It's a matter of life and death."

"You are in Haiti now," the driver replied. "The police is . . . how can I say . . . very occupied. Perhaps I can help you. Can I help you with your problem?"

Kevin caged the annoying thoughts and set his mind on accomplishing his mission. He considered the driver's taut visage, the heat-yellowed eyes, and the sweat beading the man's temples. He took in his surroundings, tracing with his sharp mind every inch of terrain. Children wailed from behind a great fence, begging for alms to be dropped into their hands.

"My friend," Kevin said, "I need to find a family."

"Yes." There was confidence in the driver's voice.

"Have you ever heard of a certain Florestant family?"

The driver rubbed the stubble on his chin, then he raised his eyes, searching the air. "Many Florestant families live here," he allowed. "Many. Some rich, some poor. Some black, some mulatto. Same name, different family. You understand?"

Kevin thought about how Jacqueline liked to tell him that in her beloved country "family" comprised every single blood kin—living or dead—from the beginning of time to forever. Of course, they would be as related as all the Smiths, Joneses, and Williamses in the United States. "The wife's name is Annette, her husband is Paul. Florestant. Heard of them?"

The driver nodded. "Ah, my friend, you are talking about the most important Florestant here." He adjusted the rearview mirror for a better look at his passenger. "My wife works in the marketplace, not far from the Breadfruit House. We know that family very well. They're in the hills. I know exactly where their house is. They must have a thousand breadfruit trees up there."

"Can you take me there?" Kevin asked, flashing a fifty-dollar bill.

"*Naturellement*," the driver replied, pulling out of the airport's parking lot.

Kevin rang the bell several times in quick succession. When no one came to the gate, he pounded it with the same brutality he had unleashed against his enemies in the desert. The metal gate, which had been baking in the ruthless Caribbean sun all day, burned his hand.

Ordinarily, Pachou would have opened the gate and berated whomever dared disrespect the Florestant property in such a brazen way. Today, he and the maids were on the porch, not wanting to be distracted lest one of Annette's commands went ignored.

"Jacqueline!" Kevin bellowed, his voice shaking with anger. "Amber!" He noticed the blocks missing from the wall on the other side of the property, creating holes large enough for an entire army to pass through. *Is this what Jacqueline considers a fort?* he asked himself. He went in.

When he reached the porch one of the maids asked, *"Monsieur, vous êtes qui?"*

"Is Jacqueline here?" he asked in English.

"Un moment."

The maid entered the living room and reported that an American was on the porch asking for Jacqueline. Annette shot Paul a look that told him to stay put.

When she saw Kevin, she opened her arms to embrace him. He pushed past her. She let her arms fall.

Kevin charged into the living room. Paul looked up with a start. He opened his mouth to speak, but there were no words. Kevin yelled Amber's name.

In her bedroom, Jacqueline made fists and pounded her face and head. Leyla grabbed her hands, speaking to her in a soft voice, smoothing her hair. "What happened is not your fault. You have to believe that it was just a terrible accident."

They waited for Kevin, like two kidnapped victims waiting for their torturer or deliverer. He charged into the room like a wounded lion, roaring: "Where's Amber?"

Jacqueline doubled over and screamed.

EIGHTEEN

At the airport, Jacqueline resisted the urge to howl like someone being burned alive. Leyla held her friend's hand. Kevin followed a few steps behind, his mouth set, his eyes wet and swollen. Behind him, Annette's heels click-clacked on the concrete. Paul's face was contorted with grief.

The shards of glass cutting through Jacqueline's throat made breathing almost impossible. The voices inside her head asked the same questions: *How could you have left your child with Annette? You always warned Amber about talking to strangers, but you delivered her into the arms of one. Amber did not ask for the moon. She wanted only to see the covey of birds. You couldn't give her such a small gift? How could you have been so lazy? How could you have been so selfish? You did this, Jacqueline. You did this to your own child.*

Kevin's mind drifted so far out of his body that he did not know when the plane took off in Port-au-Prince nor when it landed at Baltimore-Washington International Airport. The flight might have lasted four hours, four seconds, or four hundred years; he couldn't tell. Now that he had come back to the States—to lay Amber to rest—he wanted to run back to the desert. He craved the feeling of advancing into enemy territory unarmed, knowing that each step would be his last. He wanted to die.

The taxi ride from the airport was dreadful. The anguish was tangible. It was the beginning of the end. Amber had come back with them, but she was not *with* them. Annette had wanted Amber in the Florestant family's towering mausoleum, but Kevin refused vehemently. He wanted Amber in the United States, where she belonged. She never should have left her home in the first place. Had she stayed where she was supposed to be all along, she would be alive now.

Paul agreed with Annette, and thought it would have been best to keep Amber with the other Florestant family members in the mausoleum.

"You had her in your hands for five seconds and you could not take care of her," Kevin had snarled.

Kevin did not want the Florestants in his home, but knew that asking them to leave would create a problem he did not need. When they were in the kitchen, he barricaded himself in the bedroom. When they were in the living room, he went out into the hallway, pacing back and forth. At night he went to a bar, letting his mind wander. He did not want them treading on the same floor where Amber used to run into his arms. He could hear her voice still, calling out to him. He could feel the softness of her cheeks as he wiped away her tears.

Again, his mind drifted back to the desert, except this time he wanted the rifle aimed at his heart. He wanted to die alone, just as Amber had died alone. Children should not die alone. Children should not die. Parents should not outlive their babies.

Jacqueline locked herself in the bathroom. Her body shivered with grief. She vomited. She struck her head with her fist, but the image of Amber's lifeless body would not retreat. She wondered if Amber was comfortable. She did not want to think of her baby all alone in that place where she was being "prepared" for the inevitable.

She lifted her head toward the ceiling, hoping to hear a word from the God she had once loved. One second she begged Him to take back what had happened, the next she cursed Him for allowing a child to drown in the first place. She dropped to her knees and brought her face to the ground, then vomited and lay in her own mess, praying feverishly one second, spewing expletives the next.

She cursed her parents. She cursed Haiti, and she cursed herself. She cursed Kevin for not stopping her from going. She cursed him for not going with her. Had he been there, he would have taken Amber to see the peacocks. He would have held her hand the entire time. They would have been safe. Kevin, then, was to blame.

NINETEEN

Jacqueline had not returned to church since the incident with Sister Marsha and the hymnal. The pastor recognized her right away, but said nothing about Jacqueline's prolonged absence from church. She understood why Jacqueline had stayed away: she was embarrassed for what she had done. Several members of the congregation held grudges; thought she was not welcome in this house of God. They both knew it.

Jacqueline sat before Sister Marsha now, crumpled and tear-stained. Kevin sat nearby, his arms folded on his chest; his legs crossed away from her. The only reason he had accompanied Jacqueline was so he could leave the house where his in-laws were constantly lurking. He wished they had stayed in Haiti where they belonged, or in a hotel. He sat motionless as Sister Marsha began speaking.

"I won't say that I understand your pain, but there's no doubt you're going through a difficult time."

Jacqueline looked at Kevin and nodded. His face was like a freshly painted wall: blank, giving away nothing.

"It is okay to cry. No need to try and be strong for anybody right now, sweetheart. You need to express all that stuff inside of you. Let it out."

Jacqueline covered her face with her hands and wept.

Sister Marsha continued in a lulling tone: "Years ago, my older brother got involved with the wrong people. They came looking for him one night. They knocked on my door, yelling for him to come out. I told them he was not in. They broke in anyway. My son, just five years old at the time, hid in the hall closet when he heard the commotion. They barged in, heard some movement in the closet, and shot several rounds. When they opened the door and saw it was my son they had killed, they told me they were sorry. Just like that. They told me they would not come back unless my brother crossed them again. They told me my brother was lucky. I wanted to kill them. I wanted to kill my brother for getting involved with those kinds of people. I knew people who could have avenged my son. I could have paid just the right amount of money and gotten revenge, but that would not have brought my son back. Besides, something else took control of my thoughts. Something bigger filled the emptiness in my heart. The Lord filled me with the sweet assurance that He would take the pain from me."

Jacqueline reached for Kevin's hands. He pretended not to notice.

"*Death is but a transition from a world where joys decline. To the realm of eternal life where thine endless glories shine.* Let us now discuss the home-going service for Amber."

Jacqueline sniffled. Kevin looked away, not wanting to hear another word—Amber was not going "home." On the contrary, she had left home and was lost among billions of other lost people. Strangers. He would never locate her in the dark place where she was now. If only he knew where to look, he would plunge into the abyss to find her. He had visited the dark, bottomless chasm sev-

eral times, to pry soldiers out of its murky estuary before
it swallowed them completely. Kevin had heard about the
supposed bright beacon illuminating the path to eternity,
but he knew there had to be only darkness. There was
no receiving line made up of long-lost family members.
There was only the void. Absolute oblivion that spun like
a web, trapping the dead like spiders trapping flies.

Something hot rushed through Kevin's tear ducts. His
body was in a house of worship, but his mind was back
in the desert. He hoisted the M-16 up to shoulder level,
keeping a steady index finger on the trigger. His eyes
scanned the space around him carefully, taking in the
shape of every bullet hole in a concrete wall a few feet
away. He moved swiftly, knowing at any moment one
of the faceless enemies could rise out of the dust and
kill him. Tears were dangerous and could get a soldier
killed by enemy fire, friendly fire, or both. So he steadied
himself and let the rage surge through him—rage was
required in war.

Kevin knew the God who brought him home from the
war could be shrewd too. One had to be careful how one
dealt with Him. He did not like to be imposed upon. He
grew frustrated and impatient with petitioners who refused to budge, even when He gave them proof after proof
that their favor would not be granted. They went on, begging and pleading until their vocal chords snapped. They
humiliated themselves, crying out, *Please, please, please-
pleaseplease*, and, *Give me, give me, give me this, just this once*. God
did not appreciate being begged—Kevin had learned that
long ago.

Amber had fallen into the bottomless ravine, and he
could not reach her. God knew just how to get her back,

but would He? Amber was gone. Kevin would have to accept that.

Hours bled into one another, stretching toward eternity, until the funeral arrangements for Amber were finalized. Choking back sobs, Jacqueline whispered, "I never thought this day would come."

Kevin could not tell her he felt the same. He did not know what he felt. He was hollow inside. There were no rivulets of blood flowing within him, carrying memories and life; there was no heart beating, keeping him alive; there were no thoughts in his mind now. Everything had become nothing. And nothing at all mattered.

TWENTY

Annette wore a black couture jacket and a pencil skirt. The wide-brimmed hat with a black veil added a second shield to her extra-dark sunglasses. Her hair was pulled back tightly and held together at the nape of her neck with a baroque-style clasp. Her pearls shone in stark contrast to the well-worn wooden pews. Jacqueline wore one of her too-long black dresses.

Kevin sank into his seat, bearing his grief as courageously as he had borne the desert. The sorrow that would one day besiege him now stood in the air like the acrid smell of embalmment fluid. The grief which would settle on his face one day had yet to assume a shape. He felt cold and hot at the same time. He worried about Amber. He wished he had brought her favorite Little Mermaid blanket. She was cold; he was sure of it. He chided himself for being so forgetful.

Jacqueline's head throbbed. The thick smell of incense—and the hurricane of memories inside her body—threatened to suffocate her.

Dominating the sanctuary was none other than the Christ. His frame—made in mosaic—took up the entire north wall. His bare torso was broad and muscular like seven Mr. Universe winners combined. This powerfully built Christ did not look like the meek kind who gave himself willingly to save a lost world. This One looked more lion than lamb.

Jacqueline stared at the image in amazement. She wondered who the artist was that created this exquisite Christ: those thousands of pieces of glass had to be positioned just right. One mistake and the blue tiles could have dimmed the eyes' reflective glimmer, making them appear myopic and downcast.

Christ's gaze reached deep into Jacqueline, questioning her, admonishing her, punishing her. She held His gaze for a moment before lowering her own eyes. He blamed her for Amber's accident, she was sure of it. She was culpable. Scalding tears filled her eyes, but, in the silence of her heart, she asked one question: *Why did you allow me to drop Amber's umbilical cord into the river?*

Jacqueline now wished she had traveled to Haiti and put Amber's *kòd lonbrit* underneath the oldest breadfruit tree on the Florestant property. If anyone other than Annette had advised her to do that, she might have. If Leyla had been the one who told her to put the child's *kòd lonbrit* under a tree, she would certainly have done it. But Leyla came into her life long afterward.

Jacqueline reached for Kevin's hand. He looked at her trembling fingers, then turned away as if they were diseased. The woman singing "Ave Maria" stood rigidly, as though she were conserving her energy for a more portentous occasion. The church's schedule listed Amber's as the first of three home-going services that day.

"*Ave Maria Gratia plena,*" the woman sang.

Everyone turned to look at the two pallbearers walking solemnly toward the bier. Each footstep was like a peal of thunder. Jacqueline reached for Kevin's hand again. He still refused to touch her.

"*Maria Gratia plena,*" the woman sang as the men lifted the lacquered white coffin with gloved hands. "*Maria Gratia plena,*" the woman raised her voice to confirm what everyone knew: one day it would be their turn inside a shiny box that would be lifted up and carted away without them knowing.

Paul stood and tried to steady himself on his prosthetic limbs that came with a ten-year warranty. Instinctively, Annette slid her arm around his waist, keeping him upright.

The singing woman gave a subtle hand signal, prompting the organist to change chords. It was time to sing the dirge reserved for the slow march from the church to the hearse. The great-grandparents Amber had never known were now waiting with open arms to embrace her and introduce her to those who had come before them and the ones before that; they would escort their progeny all the way back to the Creation. She would learn the secret to why some babies insisted on being born feet first.

"*How great Thou art . . .*" The soloist's voice was a dying ember under a heap of sodden ashes.

Annette opened her mouth, and what came out was a soprano that promised the living that their miracle was just around the bend. The hired singer's eyes darted about, scanning the sanctuary for the one outperforming her. When she saw who it was, she threw her wet-charcoal voice even higher.

Paul moved slowly, unsteadily toward the exit. As they neared the door, Annette stopped singing and emitted a series of unintelligible utterances. All the languages she spoke came bubbling up, but not a word was comprehensible. Jacqueline doubled over as she moaned. Kevin did not hold her. Leyla rushed toward her friend, keeping her from collapsing.

The singer waited until the all mourners had left the sanctuary to belt out the last note. Her voice was too weak to usher them onto the street, but within the four walls of stained glass and holiness, she was the brightest and only star.

They drove to the cemetery in the limousine that came with the home-going service package. Sister Marsha was already there, like a hostess awaiting the arrival of dignitaries. She said a prayer, arms extended over the yawning earth. The pastor invited those gathered to take a flower from a wreath and toss it over the coffin. Afterward, the pastor scooped dirt from around the open grave and threw it onto the coffin. Then she asked everyone to do the same. As soon as the grains of earth connected with the coffin, Jacqueline let out a wail that threatened to awaken every other being in the ground. Paul and Annette threw their flowers in and shoveled dirt into the hole. Hot tears bubbled in Kevin's eyes.

Jacqueline watched her husband out of the corner of her eye. She could feel his heart breaking. When she reached for him, for the first time since the accident, Kevin took her hand. She put her head on his shoulder and her tears fell in globs on his sleeve. The sun's heat beat on their enflamed faces. The fragrance from the profusion of gladioli and carnations in the wreaths filled her nostrils. Her eyes were open, but she saw nothing.

There would be no *repas* afterward. There would be no

celebration, only grief. Paul and Annette offered to stay with Jacqueline and Kevin for a few days after the funeral, but Kevin insisted that they leave. "We'll be fine," he told them.

Leyla offered to bring food to the apartment; Kevin refused without a thank you. Grief had a way of binding people into convoluted knots; he and Jacqueline had too heavy a weight on their marriage now to entertain outsiders.

TWENTY-ONE

Nine months had passed since Amber's accident. Nine months since Jacqueline had even looked at a canvas. The memories of her trip to Haiti were still raw.

She dialed the number which she had tried a thousand times to forget but never would. Annette answered. Jacqueline regretted making the call instantly, but she needed to speak with her parents today.

In all the months since Kevin had told the Florestants to leave their apartment, Jacqueline had spoken to her parents a grand total of three times. She gave them excuse after excuse for being unable to talk. She took pride in playing the part of the daughter whose parents had forgotten to raise her. Today, she would not pretend to be brave. She needed her family.

Annette listened dutifully as secrets flew out of Jacqueline's mouth like unfed spirits. She told her how her marriage had wilted, like the flowers Kevin delivered to Amber's grave every day.

"We talked about trying to have another child," Jacqueline confessed. She omitted the part about Kevin losing interest in trying, as well as him losing interest in staying married to the woman he blamed for the greatest loss of his life. "The pastor recommended counseling, but Kevin doesn't believe in that sort of thing." His resentment ran too deep for counseling sessions. Instead, he said he had only one question he wanted answered: *Where were you when our daughter fell in the pool?*

Their marriage had become an infected sore that had to be excised. The last time Jacqueline saw Kevin, he slammed the door on his way out. She felt then she might never see him again. His heart was too busy breaking to contemplate reconciliation.

"He filed for divorce," Jacqueline explained. Her voice was gravelly and her breathing labored. She imagined her mother peering at the breadfruit trees in the yard, thinking about Amber's *kòd lonbrit*. "Are you there?" Jacqueline asked in a frail voice. "*Manman*, are you there?"

Annette inhaled deeply. "I'm here," she replied, then added, "Someone has been waiting to speak to you for a long time now."

A few seconds later, Jacqueline heard her father's voice. "How is my beautiful daughter?" he asked.

"I've been better."

"Just tell me what you need. I'll make it happen."

Jacqueline plagiarized herself, repeating verbatim what she had said to her mother, minus the deluge of tears.

"I always liked Kevin," Paul admitted.

"You don't have to lie," Annette whispered in the background.

The voice was muffled, but Jacqueline heard her father tell her mother to close her mouth in a not-so-civil manner. That lifted the corners of her own mouth into a smile.

"Our friend who runs Baybrook Hospital in Miami knows someone who owns an orphanage in Haiti," Paul

began. "He gets these children, you see. I'll give him a call.
A little girl, a little boy, or both—it's up to you. I'd take
care of everything. All you would need to do is choose one
who pleases you. From start to finish, the entire process
wouldn't take more than a few weeks. And it would be
yours."

Jacqueline held the telephone away from her ear and
stared at it blankly. She recalled an article about a couple
from Pennsylvania who had adopted a boy in the quake's
aftermath. One of the parents had boasted on social me-
dia that her new Haitian adoptee's first English words
were: *The Philadelphia Eagles rule!* Jacqueline had questioned
how it was possible for these adoptions to take place so
swiftly. The number of children being taken out of the
country was disturbing. Everyone was so stunned by the
tragedy that all they could do was praise these winged
beings who swooped down from all corners of the sky to
rescue Haiti's orphans. There hadn't been time to question whether or not the adoptions were even legal. Every
day, it seemed, there was a new story about Haiti's children being distributed to families throughout the world.
Europe and North America scored the highest.

Here she was now, listening to her father's anxious
breathing as he waited for her response. What came out
of Jacqueline's mouth was, "That's outrageous, illegal,
immoral, and tantamount to kidnapping."

"Not at all," Paul assured her in a voice that wavered
only slightly. "I wouldn't have mentioned it if there was a
doubt about the adoption being illegitimate. These poor
children's parents died in the earthquake or its aftermath.
No other family member has claimed them. Nobody wants
these kids. We'd be doing a good deed."

Jacqueline suppressed the tears. The notion of having a child in her arms again caused her heart to jump.

Paul continued in a tentative tone: "You need time to think, I know. When you decide, come back here. Bring that American husband of yours. We'll go to the orphanage together. It's not far—"

"There is no more husband, Papa."

Paul understood. He swallowed hard. "Then you decide. Kevin will come around. I think he only wants what's best for his wife. Your happiness comes first, yes?"

"I don't want any part of it," Jacqueline intoned with little conviction.

"We would be doing a good deed," Paul repeated.

"Your feeble brain has finally crossed the bridge to insanity!" Annette shouted in the background.

Jacqueline wondered if maybe her parents were the ones who needed to acquire a child—a new child, to atone for failing to raise the one born to them. Perhaps this time, Annette would not force the new daughter to play the piano until she vomited. Perhaps she would carry her like the prow of a ship and take her to see the peacocks any time the child desired. Perhaps she would buy this new daughter show-stopping dresses and cart her around the world during summer vacations, instead of sending her to boarding school thousands of miles away. Perhaps this time her parents would be present for birthdays, Christmases, and graduation ceremonies.

"What could be more civilized? More charitable?" Paul persisted.

"If you were so caring, why didn't you save Amber?" Jacqueline heard her mother say. Annette's voice grew louder: "If your head was not so damn thick, you would have run from that crumbling store. That's the real reason why Amber is not alive today—that earthquake keeps killing people. If we had stayed in Miami instead of coming back here, Amber would not have . . ."

"I understand what you're trying to do," Jacqueline said to her father, "but I don't want any part of this."

She ended the call and sat in silence. Tears flowed down her cheeks as she contemplated the notion of having a child again. *A little girl, a little boy—or both.*

Paul closed his eyes, letting the sun's rays warm his body. Tears pooled behind his eyelids. He wished Jacqueline were home again. He would apologize for all the years he was not in her life. He would tell her the truth: it had been Annette's idea to send her to boarding school, when the president-for-life and his glamorous wife broadcasted that final party, and millions of people smelled the beautiful food that was thrown away to rot while their children starved. Annette had refused to stay in Haiti when the president was exiled and the masses began burning alive anyone they thought was associated with the former regime. It was Annette who said they were young—too young to waste their lives. She said they should enjoy life. She said there would be plenty of time to be parents in the future. Annette had said the sooner Jacqueline learned to be independent the better it would be for her. She said it was for her own good. *Please, forgive your father for that. Please, forgive your mother too.*

TWENTY-TWO

Jacqueline was ten years old again. Her father picked her up from school one afternoon. When they reached the porch, they found Pachou with his hands pressed over his mouth. Blood seeped between his fingers, drenching the collar and front of his denim shirt. His eyes were wild with rage and shock. A scream died in Jacqueline throat. There were splashes of blood on the white wicker chairs and on the floorboards.

Paul rushed to Pachou and asked what happened. Pachou tried to speak through the searing pain, but could not lift his tongue. Annette stood on the opposite side of the porch, the handle of a knife clutched firmly in her right hand. There was blood on her elegant skirt and on the white buttons of her linen blouse.

"That'll teach you to spread rumors about my family!" Annette roared. "That'll teach you to smear shit on the Florestant name again! Your mother was a maid at this house, don't you ever forget that. I let you live on this property because I feel sorry for you. Let my parents rest in peace or I swear I will kill you. Do you hear me?"

Pachou just stood there quivering. The pain in his eyes was beyond physical. It was an ancient hurt—something passed down from many generations.

Paul put the groundskeeper in his car and drove as

fast as he could to the nearest hospital. The doctor saw Pachou right away, understanding that the patient was brought in by Paul Florestant. The doctor did not ask how the injury occurred, and Paul didn't volunteer an explanation. How fortunate the young man was to be in the Florestant family's employ. Another employer might have ignored the wound and let him bleed to death. Now, thanks to Paul, the man would live. His speech would always be impaired, but otherwise he would have a normal life.

Jacqueline never talked about that incident, but she never forgot it either. She would always recall Pachou's blood trickling through the cups his hands had made to cover his mouth. She had feared her mother would wield the bloodstained knife and attack her right there on the porch too. But Annette had simply put the knife down, gone into the house, and taken a long bath. By nightfall, the household was as calm as always. The Florestant family sat in the salon. Annette sipped Grand Marnier, Paul read a journal, and Jacqueline played "Fantaisie Impromptu" as she had never played before.

While Pachou stood bleeding, Annette had seen the horror in Jacqueline's eyes, and feared the child would grow up hating her. That was the moment she decided to send her to a boarding school in the United States. Not to mention, her *belle époque* had come to an abrupt end. The president-for-life and his beautiful wife had been swooped away and exiled, leaving their friends and supporters to fend for themselves. Annette and Paul feared retribution from the judges, juries, and executioners chanting together in the sweltering streets of Port-au-Prince.

They sent Jacqueline to a prestigious boarding school

five thousand miles away. The school offered unmatched academics, along with equestrian, ballet, music, and visual art programs. Jacqueline did not care much for horses; ballet bored her. She had played the piano until she became physically ill, and as such refused to touch another musical instrument. Art was the last option, so she learned to embrace it.

Jacqueline became fluent in English in just a few months. Teachers adored her. Some wondered why Mr. and Mrs. Florestant never attended teacher-parent conferences, but most of them understood it was not unusual for parents to be too busy with their personal lives to visit. Jacqueline was one of many students who stayed on campus during holidays, including summer vacations.

During the first year at boarding school, she cried in her sleep, but resentment soon filled her heart, leaving no space for self-pity. She learned not to look around the room hoping to see Annette and Paul during award ceremonies. She learned to forget the shapes of their eyes.

By the time Jacqueline graduated from high school, she did not care if she saw Paul or Annette ever again. But they came for the ceremony, dressed in fine clothes and bearing flowers as ornate as funeral wreaths. Annette expected Jacqueline to return to Haiti with them that summer, and then she would travel to Paris to attend university, as her parents had arranged.

Jacqueline was seventeen years of age at the time. She told her parents that the decision to stay in the United States or return to Haiti was now hers to make. Annette thought about several fascinating countries she had yet to visit and said, "We'll trust you to behave like a responsible young lady. Of course we will pay for your college tuition, housing, and make sure you have enough spending money. Cash is the last thing Paul and I would want you to worry about."

"I received a scholarship," Jacqueline had said. "I also have a part-time job."

"Well, of course you got a scholarship," Annette beamed with maternal pride, "you are naturally brilliant—you are a Florestant."

"Will you live on campus?" Paul inquired. "Do you want us to find a suitable place for you to live? We have friends who—"

"I plan to live on campus," Jacqueline interrupted.

"In that case, it's settled," Annette proclaimed. Jacqueline knew what she meant, and this time she did not argue.

Every month, like a salaried employee, Jacqueline received a money transfer from her parents. *For living expenses*, they wrote. Jacqueline's part-time job paid a small salary; luckily, her only luxury was gourmet coffee. She put away the money her parents sent, and later used it to purchase outright the apartment where she still lived. Paul and Annette continued to send money, but Jacqueline never touched it. The money stayed in a bank account, growing like an overfertilized garden.

Undergraduate and graduate schools took six years in total—a time during which Jacqueline did not see her parents, although they spoke on the phone now and again. Paul and Annette continued traveling around the world, shopping for priceless crystals to give to friends, taking pictures of themselves in front of the world's wonders, sending postcards from foreign ports.

When Jacqueline informed her parents that she had

married an American in a civil ceremony, Annette was so infuriated she did not speak to her daughter for months.

The next time she saw her parents, it was after Amber was born. That was also when they first met Kevin.

"He's some sort of soldier," Annette had said to Paul. "He looks like a brute."

"He's a Marine," Jacqueline explained, "and he is not a brute."

"I don't like him," Annette declared. "What kind of man marries a girl without asking her father's permission?"

Jacqueline had laughed bitterly. "Can you repeat that?" When Annette pursed her lips and turned away, Jacqueline asked another question: "What kind of mother leaves her only child in the hands of strangers for years, without coming by once to see if the child is alive or dead?" That was the end of their conversation about Kevin.

During the months after Amber's birth, Jacqueline covered canvas after canvas with scenes from a Baltimore City that flourished only in her imagination. The streets were lined with lush shrubs. Children flew colorful kites in parks. Couples pushed prams with perfect babies in them. Lovers, enveloped in dense fog, held hands on suspended bridges.

Jacqueline joined an artist co-op where painters displayed their work for a small fee. She sold a piece here and there, but it wasn't anything she could live on. When she heard that a nearby school was looking for an art teacher, she applied. Surely there were Rembrandts, O'Keefes, Basquiat, and at least one Catharine Peace among the city's children. Surely there were protégés whose potential might go unnoticed unless she stepped into life's ring and played referee to keep the city's many dangers from pulverizing the kids and sending them to early graves. She took the job happily and taught for several years. The teachers and students adored her. The principal did not, but there weren't many people apart from himself for whom he cared.

Now the earthquake and the accident in her parents' pool had changed everything. She could no longer paint, and she could not teach. She could barely breathe. Jacqueline fought back the only way she knew, spiking her morning coffee with scotch and turning Foula's vodou jazz music up so loud the walls shook. When those measures failed to work, she attacked Kevin's fix-all pills in the medicine cabinet. He had been in such a hurry to leave, he had left his bucket of gold behind. Jacqueline assumed he was acquiring more from his friend Michael Baker. Kevin would not move forward in life without his precious pills.

Jacqueline had no way of knowing that when Kevin had tried to restock his supply, Michael Baker surprised him with news of his own.

"What are you talking about?" Kevin asked.

"I mean, I can't do this shit anymore."

"Do what?"

"These pills, man. I'm done. I can't do this shit anymore."

"That's cool," Kevin had said, even though it wasn't. "What happened?"

"Got a good thing going with this new girl I met. She served overseas too, man. She knows how it is."

"Yeah?"

"Yeah. She hooked me up with this, uh, facility. They got all kinds of doctors. I can talk to these people. Half of them are vets, they know the deal . . ."

Kevin listened as Michael went on, nodding occasionally. Of course he could find a different supplier, that would be easy enough. But Michael's new revelation changed their relationship. They seldom communicated as it was; now, there would be no reason to have any conversation. As Michael talked more about getting help, something inside Kevin shifted. For the first time since he had come back from the desert, he considered what life might be like without that intruder always waking him up in the middle of the night, hiding inside his closet, waiting for him at his office at work, telling him to get out of his car, step over the railing, and discover the secret city the government had built underneath the Chesapeake Bay.

"Anyway, I'm done with these pills. I'm clean, I want a life. Anything's got to be better than sleeping all day long. I'm sick of myself. Know what I mean, man?"

TWENTY-THREE

"*S*addle *my horse, somebody, I'm leaving soon*," Jacqueline half-sang the Boucon Ginen song and half-sobbed as she lashed at a canvas one afternoon. The easel trembled under the furious brushstrokes. The relentless roar of the drums could not distract her. She went to the balcony and looked below, contemplating what might happen if she just ended it all. But she would never do that. Her *kòd lonbrit* under that breadfruit tree had become one with the earth, and if the earthquake that nearly destroyed Haiti had not touched those trees, she would survive too.

For months the neighbors had not complained about the drums shaking their walls and interrupting their sleep. They knew about Amber's accident. They had watched through peepholes as Kevin stormed out of Jacqueline's life. People talked, and the puzzle was not that difficult to assemble. Some of the neighbors wondered what they would have done if the same thing happened to them. But it had been almost a year already; surely they were entitled to a little rest. Now, when Jacqueline's music thundered in the middle of the night, the neighbors would walk right up to her door and knock. They used to say, *Please turn it down*. Lately, no one said please anymore.

A heavy rain was falling when the Foula CD stalled on *"Sen Jak pa la. Chen an ki la. Chen an mode mwen . . ."*

Jacqueline charged toward the CD player and flung it across the room. Her head jerked with panic when her phone rang. She stared at it, uncertain of how to proceed.

"What's going on?" Leyla's voice sounded overly calm. "I've left a hundred voice messages. Sent you millions of texts and e-mails. I've been so worried about you. Where have you been?"

"I kept meaning to check my phone," Jacqueline said by way of an apology. She was both relieved and annoyed that Leyla had called. One part of her wanted to tell her friend she did not have time to talk; another longed to disclose the particulars she'd told no one since Kevin left.

She had not left her apartment in many weeks. She cried all the time. She had not slept in days. She had started painting again, but could not seem to transfer a simple image from her mind to the canvas. Her imagination was now a womb of toxins. She thought about teaching again, but asked herself how she could help students when she had failed to help her only child. Besides, the students' horror stories would overwhelm her. Perhaps she would return to the classroom one day. Not now.

"I've organized a little gathering in honor of my favorite artist," Leyla said in a cheerful voice. "Nothing major. Just a couple of friends at my place."

"It's too soon," Jacqueline replied. "I'm not ready for parties."

"It won't be a party," Leyla said. "I want to showcase your work, draw some interest from the appropriate people. You never know what might happen."

"It's too soon."

"You'll be great. I told them you're amazing. Don't make a liar out of your best friend."

When the call ended, Jacqueline opened her e-mail account and found hundreds of messages. She opened only the ones from Leyla, starting with the oldest. As Jacqueline read, golden sunrays filled the apartment and threw their reproach across the piles of laundry that doubled as beds whenever sleep claimed her.

Jacqueline felt a sudden need to be among people. She rushed toward the front door. When she reached for the doorknob and saw the condition of her hands, she rubbed them together vigorously. Shavings of color fell to the floor. She went to the bathroom to wash and caught a glimpse of herself in the medicine cabinet's mirrored door. Her reflection startled her. The eyes that stared back were unrecognizable. The stranger looked sad and sickly—the kind of person she would have warned Amber to keep away from. *Don't talk to that woman,* she would have said.

Tears quivered in Jacqueline's eyes. She splashed cold water on her face. If only it were that simple to wash away the voice in her head constantly reminding herself of her failure as Amber's mother. She dried her face and fled the apartment like a teenage runaway.

Jacqueline walked past several restaurants before deciding to go into a deli for a sandwich. But as soon as she entered the place, the smell of food nauseated her. She ran out with the speed of a criminal. Since the funeral, she had not been so far away from Amber's room, her pillows, her toys, her clothes emblazoned with images of the Little Mermaid. Amber's bed had not been touched since the morning of June 24, when they left for Haiti.

Jacqueline picked up her mail from the lobby on her way upstairs, but didn't bother to open the envelopes, now piled in a corner like snowdrifts. She felt cold, so she pulled a sweater on top of the sweater, on top of the dress, on top of her pajamas.

For days afterward, she shivered constantly. Her skin hurt. Her lungs burned. She feared being too cold in the shower, so she stopped taking them. Her gums hurt, so she stopped brushing her teeth. Her life, like faulty scaffolding, had become unsafe; everything leaned precariously in the wrong direction, threatening to collapse. She went about like someone in whose chest beat a mechanical heart that was incompatible with her human flesh and human blood. Every breath was a boulder that had to be pushed uphill. Her defective heart kept its charge, however, ticking away like the timer on an explosive device.

When she was not sleeping, she covered canvas after canvas with strange images. She no longer differentiated red from purple, cobalt from black—colors were inconsequential. Each canvas was a little grave into which she poured a memory from the thousands that percolated in her head. A drop of paint was a broken dam, washing her clean and drowning her simultaneously. Each time a memory surfaced, she rushed to one of the canvases strewn on the floor. Her art was the life vest keeping her afloat. She lived only to paint, and painted only to live. Rest and nourishment were unimportant.

Pachou had become oddly indispensable. His likeness was there in every piece. Here he was, holding his machete against a coconut's fractured shell out of which a phantasmagorical woman appeared, hair coiled about her torso like ropes; the woman was Annette Florestant. In another piece, Annette stood behind Pachou as he scourged a breadfruit tree; she had a machete hidden behind her back. There he was again in acrylic, graphite, and oil on canvas—the contorted features were barely recognizable, but yes, it was Pachou under Annette's foot; the knife in her hand was wet, and Pachou's severed tongue was lying next to him on the ground.

One afternoon, after interring more memories onto canvas, Jacqueline stretched out on a pile of dirty laundry with her face toward the ceiling. Her eyes were open, but not seeing.

She crawled into Amber's room, moving about carefully so as not to disturb the toys. She let out a wail when she saw the silver-and-blue peacock on the wall which she had purchased from the Visionary Museum. Now she recalled that morning, months before, when the hypnotic aroma of the orchids and gardenias had filled her old bedroom in Haiti, and fate had plunged her into a darkness so profound she had yet to make her way out of it.

Jacqueline stood up and scurried out of the room. She reached for her phone, dialing hurriedly. When Leyla answered, she said it might be good for her to attend the gathering/art exhibit after all.

TWENTY-FOUR

Leyla greeted each guest warmly. She led them to the paintings on the walls and studied their faces for reactions. When Jacqueline arrived, Leyla rushed toward her with arms open. "Here she is, ladies and gentlemen," the hostess announced with a flourish of her hands, "my favorite artist, Jacqueline Florestant."

"That's quite a painting," someone remarked of the piece dominating the room, which Jacqueline had painted when she'd first received the CD from Leyla and the drum music had filled the apartment and her heart. The music had delivered to her a singular childhood memory which guided her fingers, letting her know precisely how much of each tint she needed to recreate that iridescent mosaic under the Caribbean Sea. Her own eyes had stared back from the liquid mirror, as if from a dream. Sitting in her parents' friend's shiny yacht, spellbinding circles had invited her to come on under. *Dive right in, why don't you, dear? Behold this marvel from within, and sob. Come see with your own eyes what the Pinzon brothers had seen in 1492, when the island was an untouched virgin, blameless as a pearl in an oyster's shell.* Jacqueline recalled the day she held onto the side of that yacht while she looked into the land mass forming below, mesmerized by the colors that whispered her name and promised the eternal. That hypnotic world under the sea now stared back at her from the painting on the wall. That indescribable thing she had seen under the water was the same that used to twirl her around her kitchen island. The fancy boat had rocked gently above the mosaic that was as beautiful as the powerfully built Christ in Sister Marsha's sanctuary.

The colors can draw you under, the captain had said with an odd laugh. *Hold on tight, young miss.* His eyes were the sepia of experience, his breath heavy with rum, but he held hers in a steady gaze. *Hold on, no matter what you might see below.*

Standing before Leyla's guests caused the soft flesh under Jacqueline's eyes to throb—just as it had long ago in the church, right before she hurled the hymnal at the unsuspecting pastor. Needles stabbed at her temples. Her hands and the spaces between her toes were slick with sweat. Her head ached. A breadfruit plunged from her throat to the bottom of her stomach and threatened to come up again—whole—making it difficult to breathe.

Jacqueline excused herself and rushed to the bathroom. She leaned over the sink and waited for the memory of everything she had eaten in her life to come up in a great, sacrilegious wave—but nothing happened. She came out of the bathroom unsure of which direction to turn. She went to the kitchen, advancing cautiously. She hoped she would not be scolded like a child.

"Lost, miss?" It was Leyla.

"What gave me away?" Jacqueline felt uncomfortable in her skin. The thicket of hair covering her head made her look like a terrified waif.

Leyla eyed her with a good measure of sympathy. "You're not enjoying the party?"

"I am," Jacqueline lied, and apologized for not playing the guest of honor part properly. She told Leyla she didn't feel well.

"Go hang out in my room for a little while. I'm sure everyone will understand. I'll be up in a bit."

Dozens of tiny insects pricked Jacqueline's pores. There was a shrill ringing in her ears, a continuous gong in her skull. "I'll just go back home. You mustn't leave your guests to entertain themselves."

Leyla nodded quietly.

TWENTY-FIVE

As soon as Jacqueline returned to the apartment, she went into Amber's room and sat on the bed. She could hear Paul playing his lifeless "Fantaisie Impromptu." She saw before her the heap of condolence cards with gaping holes in the clouds and stairways arching toward the sun. She recalled Kevin screaming and slamming the door on his way out of her life. She remembered Sister Marsha asking everyone to shovel dirt at the cemetery. She heard Amber scream for Grandmère to take her to see the peacocks. A black fog settled low in the room and enveloped her. She curled her legs under her body and slept.

Jacqueline called Paul at daybreak. He was thrilled to hear from his daughter after so long a silence. "Papa . . ." Her voice broke.

"Yes?"

"What happened was nobody's fault. Don't blame yourself."

Paul exhaled. "I went to the orphanage just the other day," he blurted out, in spite of himself. "There's a little girl there, two years old. She doesn't have anyone. The orphanage is legitimate. My friend's dealings are legitimate. He takes care of these kids no one wants."

"Arranging illegal adoptions is not what normal people do."

"You misunderstand, Jacqueline. My friend is not a criminal. He does not sell children. Some of these kids are left on his doorstep. The man could be living a great life anywhere in the world, but chooses instead to care for other people's discarded children."

After the conversation with her father, Jacqueline picked up the makeshift beds from around her apartment and washed the clothes that had been waiting to see soap and water for ages.

Annette stopped speaking to Paul for weeks when she learned that Pachou had driven him to the orphanage several times. During the first drive, the two of them discussed the children no one seemed to want.

"There are orphans all around the world," Paul said, remembering his visits to poor nations in other hemispheres. He recalled the indigents in Calcutta and Gorkha. "You should have seen the poverty there."

Pachou could not believe there were places in the world where people were as poor as Haitians. Paul assured him that there were, and said he would show Pachou the photographs.

"I will not disagree with you," Pachou said. "But there is another problem that is just as bad, in my opinion."

"What is that?" Paul asked.

"This is a problem that turn rich people into poor ones."

"I give up."

"Thieves in fancy suits who steal land from people. They come with fake papers and lie to the poor man who doesn't know he's really rich. They take the land our ancestors left us, and leave us in shacks that blow like burnt matchsticks in the hurricane. Big companies from all over the world come here and buy our land for pennies. They're not the worst, though. I blame them, but I don't blame them. Do you know what I mean?"

Paul nodded.

"Family—our relatives—are the ones who hurt us the most. They steal acres and acres and sell them behind the rightful owners' backs. There are no laws to stop them."

"You have a point," Paul said. "Foreigners are not supposed to buy land in Haiti, but there are loopholes. And if they have money to pay the right people, those loopholes get wider by the dollar . . . There'll come a day when Haitian people will have to rent a place to live from a foreign national. They're taking over every inch of the country with their forts. Mark my words: I'd like to see them try to put their hands on my property," Paul pumped his fists in the air.

"I am not talking about foreigners stealing land," Pachou replied. Paul looked at him askance. "When it's your own blood who steals your inheritance, that's even worse."

Paul realized where the conversation was headed, and tried to change it. But Pachou would not be deterred.

"I know how you feel about the aid workers, Paul, but they're not all bad. Some of them have good intentions. There's this organization that gives free lawyering to people like me, you understand? They fill out the right forms. They stand before judges and plead our cases. They help people get back land that was stolen from them."

"Where is this conversation leading, Pachou?"

"So far they've helped a lot of people get back what is rightfully theirs."

"That's good, I suppose."

"Yes, it is good," Pachou said. "That's what I call a miracle in this country."

"I don't exactly believe in miracles."

"I didn't either. But I do now. They've helped many people I know. They've helped *me*."

"How is that?" Paul asked.

"That morning when I found Amber in the pool, I was on my way to a very important meeting. I had to miss it, of course, but the organization understood. They gave me and my case a second chance. They are very smart people. Haitians, you know. Real lawyers who want to help, not rob people like me. They said I needed to bring proof. I told them I had plenty of that, starting with the blood in my veins. They do these tests, you know. They can find out who people are by doing something with hair or even their spit. If they drink out of a glass, all you have to do is take that glass to them and they can learn things. You can bring hair from a comb. When I tell you these people are smart, I am not kidding."

"Where are you going with this, Pachou?" Paul repeated.

"Did you ever wonder why your wife tried to cut out my tongue?"

Paul shifted in his seat.

"She said nobody would believe me anyway. And I was so scared of her, I believed her. I told myself I would live in that shack and I would wait. And one day I would find a way. And my day came."

Paul listened in silence.

"I have proof. Proof that Annette Florestant and I have

the same blood. Her father was my father. I was born on the property, as you know. My mother was a maid here. My father and her were together. Nobody knew, but my mother told me the truth. Right before she died, she told me I was a Florestant and the property was just as much mine as it was Annette's."

Paul said nothing. It was as if he had always known.

TWENTY-SIX

The Caribbean sun started healing Jacqueline as soon as her feet touched the tarmac. Paul and Annette came to fetch her from the airport. They held one another for a long time without uttering a single word.

Not a day passed without her parents telling Jacqueline how thrilled they were to have her back home, where they were certain she belonged. Annette cautioned Paul not to do or say anything that might aggrieve their daughter. Paul knew just what his wife meant; he would not mention adoption and the children who needed homes.

There was a time when Jacqueline would not have permitted Annette's maids to do anything for her. Now, she barely noticed when they brought her a meal on a tray. She liked having her breakfast waiting for her when she woke up in the morning, and lunch served at noon. She did not have to wash dishes afterward. Rest was all she was allowed to do. She needed to heal.

Late at night when Jacqueline had difficulty falling asleep, she made her way to the crumbling wall that kept her childhood home from becoming one with the ever-expanding marketplace. Pachou would join her, sitting beside her like a guardian angel on a section of the wall that was now barely a foot high.

Annette allowed Jacqueline to do anything she wanted except sit on that wall by herself late at night—like a motherless, stay-with child. That was why she asked Pachou to sit with Jacqueline.

"Anything for family," Pachou had said. "Nothing will happen to my niece while I'm there."

By now, all of Kenscoff had learned the secret which Annette had nearly cut out Pachou's tongue to keep him from revealing: her father was his father too, making him kin. He could move into the house that had been his father's house any time he wished, and Annette could not evict him. But Pachou was comfortable in his own two-room place on the property, which he'd rebuilt after the earthquake.

He let things stand as they were. But in case his sister had any doubts about his intention to remain on the property indefinitely, Pachou blocked off a parcel of land not too far from the main house and paid laborers to lay a solid foundation for the house he planned to build someday. The house would not be built for many years, but putting the foundation down let Annette know what to expect. The fact that she did nothing to stop him told Pachou what he had always known: the property and every tree on it were as much his as they were hers.

To celebrate his new status, Pachou began calling Annette Florestant by another name—*Sister*. He reminded her of all those years he'd spent scourging trees and maintaining the grounds, when he should have been sitting on a school bench learning to read and write. Laying a foundation on a section of land let Annette know that the days of her telling him what to do had ended. The last time Annette had given Pachou a command, he said,

"This property and the spirits inside the trees are as much mine as they are yours. So you do it yourself!"

Joining Jacqueline on the wall was a pleasure for Pachou, not a chore. One night as he sat beside her, he said: "The reason the Florestant family suffers so much is because Annette is evil. After my mother died, instead of sending me to school and bringing me into the house like the child I was, Annette put a machete in my hands and told me to strike the trees twenty-four times. She filled my pockets with sugar and sent me to plant melon and pumpkin seeds, saying the fruit will be sweeter if the planter's pocket is filled with sugar."

One morning during breakfast on the terrace, Annette was watching Jacqueline with maternal pride as Paul read the newspaper.

"I hate those things," Annette announced.

"What things?" Paul and Jacqueline asked in unison.

"Those breadfruit trees," Annette said. "Why don't we have them cut down?"

"They're your trees," Jacqueline said, wiping one hand with the other. "Why would you want to do that?"

Within the hour, a dozen men appeared with flatbed trucks, ropes, and chainsaws.

"Are you insane?" Paul asked his wife.

"She is," Pachou said. He went to the men preparing to remove the trees and told them their services would not be needed after all.

"We're not cutting down any trees on this property," Paul said. "The earthquake didn't bring them down, why should you?"

A breeze shook the trees' branches, as if to applaud

Paul for saving them. A ripe cherry rolled toward Annette's foot. One of the peacocks pranced over to inspect it. Annette had meant to rid the property of the covey after Amber's accident, but could not bring herself to part with them. The peacock lowered its head and sauntered back to the opposite side of the yard. The rest of the flock gathered about and lifted their trains in solidarity. Arches of opal and sapphire glimmered fiercely.

Jacqueline rose out of her chair and walked slowly to the salon, closing the door behind her. She sat on the piano bench, her posture perfect. It had been years since she had even thought about touching a piano. The memory of the music she once made descended upon her like a net of thorns. She shuddered as if cold, but realized the old repulsion was gone. Something else was taking its place. She thought about the drum songs Leyla had taught her, and began pounding on the keys. There was a fury in the notes, between them and over them.

Pachou took his place on one of the wicker throne chairs, surveying the vista his father had built.

Annette sighed. "I'd give the world for a man who could climb that tree and fetch me a good avocado this morning."

Just then, the phone rang. The maid answered and brought the phone to Paul.

"This is Paul," he said.

The voice on the other end was familiar. Affable.

"One moment," Paul said. He left the porch and moved into the living room. "It's for you."

Jacqueline had spoken to Leyla recently and did not expect her to be calling back so soon.

"It's me," the caller said.

Jacqueline froze. "Kevin?"

"I've been looking for you. Leyla said you were out of the country, so I figured you'd be at your parents' place. Listen, Jackie . . ."

"Yes?"

"I've been doing some thinking. Michael knows these people. They're no stranger to some of the stuff we all go through, know what I mean?"

"Actually, I don't."

"I've been seeing this doctor. I think there may be hope for me. For us. I want to come home."

"That sounds promising." Jacqueline's words curled into themselves like small pieces of paper set on fire.

"I miss you," Kevin said. His words gave off an ephemeral blue-gold flame that was at once dangerous and alluring.